ROYAL CATCH

KYLIE GILMORE

First Edition: May 2019

Cover design by Michele Catalano Creative

Cover photographer: David Wagner

Cover model: James Joseph

Published by: Extra Fancy Books

ISBN-10: 1-942238-84-3

ISBN-13: 978-1-942238-84-3

*Once upon a time there was a princess—
brash and bold and brave.
And not exactly a princess.*

1

Gabriel

And don't let the door hit your furry ass on the way out!

I pinch the bridge of my nose. I cannot believe my life has come to this. Me, Gabriel Rourke, the crown prince of Villroy, heir to a kingdom, kicking a furry menagerie out the palace doors. Yes, furries, people who enjoy wearing stuffed-animal suits. The kangaroo bride, koala groom, wombat minister, and way too many dingoes to count (I swear, they were multiplying) were here for a furry wedding. This is all my brother Phillip's fault. He was determined to turn the palace into a destination-wedding venue in a misguided attempt to save our faltering economy. And what happens? Furries.

Worse, every furry detail was captured by reporters from two prestigious bridal magazines, who were here to cover the inaugural non-furry wedding (that was completely botched due to the double-booking with the furries). I shudder to think what those reporters will say.

This whole wedding business is an abomination to the royal tradition, and I knew all along it was a mistake.

I haven't slept in twenty-four hours—still in my tux from the horrendous wedding travesty of last night—so when Phillip strolls into the marble entrance hall on this hellish morning, looking bright-eyed after a good night's sleep, I bark, "Where's Bonnie?"

Phillip holds up his palms. "Relax, the guards are taking care of her." I can't relax until that grossly incompetent wedding planner is gone. Clearly, Phillip can. That is the difference between being the heir and the spare. He's one year younger—the friendly, easygoing version of me —same dark brown hair and blue-green eyes, same sharp cheekbones and build.

I blow out an exasperated breath. "The woman is unhinged. You're the one who hired her. See to it she's on the next ferry." Last night I banished her from Villroy Island and ordered her to be on the first ferry out this morning.

Phillip leans in, his voice low. "Do you think there's any truth to Bonnie's story that she has royal blood? Her great-grandmother had the bastard of our great-grandfather?"

"No!" I don't want to rehash the sordid twisted story with him. Bonnie is clearly not right in the head. "I want her gone."

He lifts a hand in greeting at the non-furry bridal couple, who've just arrived in the entrance hall with their luggage, about to leave on their honeymoon. He speaks under his breath. "I need to go apologize to the happy couple for their imperfect wedding." That's putting it mildly.

I clench my jaw. Apparently, I have to do every frigging thing around here. What is taking the guards so long with Bonnie?

I stalk upstairs to the east wing, where Bonnie spent the night in a guest room with two guards posted outside her room. At this rate she's going to miss the ferry. Only one guard is waiting.

"What's taking so long?" I demand. My manners left along with my formerly dignified life.

The guard, Louis, does a quick head bow. "Your Highness, it should only be a few more minutes. Viktor had to get a few maids to help dress her."

I stare at him, incredulous. "She's taking a ferry off Villroy forever and she must dress for the occasion?"

Louis actually blushes. "She was naked. She thought to seduce us."

"Both of you?"

"Yes, sir."

The woman must be desperate. I'd almost feel sorry for her if it weren't for the terrible publicity she's brought to our family. This is the absolute last thing we need with my father, the king, in such poor health.

The door opens suddenly. Bonnie is fully dressed and subdued, her shoulders drooped as Viktor escorts her out of the room, his hand wrapped around her arm. I follow the guards downstairs. They will ride the ferry with her to ensure she leaves the island. I'm too aggravated to go to bed, so I will see this through to the bitter end.

We arrive in the entrance hall, where Phillip is still talking to the poor couple whose wedding was ruined.

The moment the palace doors close behind Bonnie, I turn to Phillip and announce loud enough for the footmen, butler, and remaining security guards to take note. "The palace is now closed to outsiders for good!"

"Gabriel, it was only one—" Phillip starts.

I cut him off. "No more weddings. No outsiders period."

The palace doors creak open and I whirl, expecting Bonnie to come racing through the doors, screaming for her right to the throne. My jaw drops at the sight before me—a young woman I've never seen before with a wild mass of dark brown curls, huge white-framed sunglasses, wearing a tight sleeveless dress with giant pineapples on it and cheetah heels.

I snap my gaping jaw shut as she leaves her wheeled suitcase by the door and hurries over to me, gesturing wildly, her voice clearly American. "I love this already!"

Before I can protest, she whips out her cell phone and snaps a picture with me.

"The palace is closed!" I bark. "And hasn't anyone ever told you it's rude to take one's photo without permission?"

She startles before muttering, "You're the rude one yelling at a guest. Geez, I flew ten hours from Tampa for this?"

Another crazy woman has breached the palace walls. "Do not speak to me of feminine products," I say through gritted teeth. "Now get out."

Someone laughs quietly nearby. I don't care. I'm too fixated on this rude intruder, who is one second from being physically removed from the premises. By me.

"Feminine?" the woman asks, cocking her head. "Oh! Ha-ha, not tampon. *Tam-pa.*" She enunciates slowly and clearly like I'm an idiot. She's the one with the accent. "That's where I just flew in from. It's a beautiful place." Her brows furrow. "I'm not sure anyone would dare call tampons beautiful."

I'm momentarily speechless.

She cups her mouth and stage-whispers behind me to the only other woman in the hall, the bride about to leave on her honeymoon, "He's a cranky butler."

I stiffen. She thinks I'm the butler? Granted, I haven't been in the public eye for several years for important reasons that I will not be going into with *her*, and I did shave my beard off, but I hadn't thought I'd aged so much as to be unrecognizable. I'm thirty years old, virile and vital. In my fucking prime!

"Who are you?" I ask in my most imperious voice.

She tosses her mass of wild dark curls over one shoulder and thrusts her hand out. "I'm Polly Lyon and that's no lie."

I stare at her hand, and my lips twitch. She's cute. Ill-mannered, but cute.

Her brown eyes flash, and she drops her hand. "You might be the hottest butler I've ever seen, but…that stick up your ass really kills it for me."

I crack a smile because she said I'm hot. I am losing it. Lack of sleep must be making me loopy, because normally this kind of insult would never slide with me. To the dungeon! Oh, yes, we have one, though it hasn't been used in centuries.

There's a shuffle behind me as the newlyweds take their leave. Phillip and two guards leave with them. I remain rooted in place, staring at the woman who had the audacity to address me, the crown prince of Villroy, heir to a fucking kingdom, as a butler. We're now alone in the entrance hall, besides the usual footmen, security guards, and the actual butler.

She plants a hand on her hip, saucy as all hell. "Are

you going to tell me your name, or should I just call you Jeeves?" She winks.

"Butler Phillip will suffice." I want to laugh, throwing my brother's name into it.

She smiles brightly, and I find myself wanting to smile back. "Just like Prince Phillip, *the* royal hottie!" she exclaims. "Much cooler than the heir to the throne. That guy, oh man, I heard he's a dud."

"A dud," I echo, hardly believing my ears.

She looks around as if to be sure the dud won't over-hear. "Yeah, a real stick-in-the mud. He never leaves the palace. There haven't even been pictures of him in years, he won't allow it. I mean, get over yourself, right?"

My jaw tightens. I am the crown prince of Villroy, my birthright, my legacy. My duty is first and foremost to the kingdom. My righteous indignation gives way to the despair that kept me up all night. The kingdom is faltering. The fishing-based economy is shaky, and the younger generation is leaving in droves. As my father's health declines and my mother refuses to take leadership without him, I know my time will soon come as king, and that means I must find a way forward for Villroy. Phillip wants to open up the palace. I, on the other hand, want to preserve our history and tradition for future generations, which means keeping the palace closed to the public. We can't have tourists running around, trampling over every-thing and destroying centuries of history. We must find another way. Only what new venture wouldn't involve outsiders? What would keep the younger generation from abandoning ship and offer them and the island a real future?

My frustrating lack of answers is the only reason I ask her, "Why exactly are you here, Polly who doesn't lie?"

She laughs. "I am here, Butler Phillip, by order of the queen. I'm Princess Mary Louise Lyon of the Beaumont Islands. Though I prefer my nickname, Polly." She taps a long red fingernail with rhinestones against her lush red lips. "I was told I'd be receiving a small inheritance."

I blanch and my gut tightens because my crafty mother has always jokingly referred to the island as our small inheritance, which means her true purpose is disturbingly clear—finding me a wife. The inheritance will be a kingdom. Polly is surely only the first in a long line of hand-picked candidates. My mother's criteria for my bride will likely be a woman with big childbearing hips. I gulp and sweat breaks out all over my body.

I've always known I would be required to marry nobility, to continue the line.

I just didn't know that time was now.

Anna

Why did I say I'm not lying? *I'm Polly Lyon and that's no lie.* Stupid guilty conscience. I'm Anna Hebert, and the truth is I'm here under false pretenses. It's for a good cause. I'm helping out my cousin Polly—a bona fide princess—who got herself in trouble back in Florida for identity theft. We're actually very distant cousins with only a great-great-great-great-great-grandfather in common. She found me through the AncestryWise website, which was awesome for both of us. For her, she'd hoped to find an American relative on her escape-to-America adventure, and for me, I was thrilled to have a cousin after growing up an orphan with no family. Though I didn't know she sought me out at first as a family ally. That all came later. She moved into the apartment next door, and we hit it off immediately. Not only do we resemble each other (we've been called twins), we're both free spirits. We became really close.

After a few months, she told me the most outlandish story—she was actually a princess in hiding from a real old-school monarchy, where her parents were pressuring her to marry a sleazy man important to her kingdom. I was understandably shocked. She'd even sounded American to my ears. (Turned out she'd picked up the accent from her posh boarding school and college in the US.) Even crazier, she told me we were distant cousins and that she'd bought the apartment building I live in when she'd first arrived to give to me as a gift, so I'd have a secure foundation after growing up an orphan. Her only request was that I let her stay as a tenant because she'd spent the money she'd brought with her on the building, and getting more funds from her homeland would alert them to her whereabouts.

Honestly, I thought it was a scam. A princess in hiding who's a long-lost relative is buying me a building? I did my research on AncestryWise and we really are related. I even got a little excited thinking maybe I could call myself a princess with my drop of royal blood, but she explained I was too far removed to be considered royal. Anyway, I accepted the gift, transferring the property to my name at her generous insistence, and I told her I'd owe her big time. I'd planned to sell the building and use the proceeds to pay for my foster dad's home nurse and open my own beauty salon. It's not a huge or luxurious building, but it's enough for my needs. Unfortunately...

Always a catch, right?

Everything came to a screeching halt when the cops

showed up and arrested Polly. She'd paid someone to get her an ID so she could get the ball rolling on her undercover life. She'd just wanted a year of freedom after college before settling down with the expected marriage and producing the royal heirs. Turned out the identity was from a deceased person, and she was found out by the very same website that had brought us together. The deceased person's aunt was building their family tree only to discover her dead niece owned property in Florida, which Polly had only bought as a gift for me. A generous yet ultimately ruinous gesture of goodwill. How can I not be loyal to her? I love this cousin of mine.

Now Polly is waiting for her court date. She could face a year of jail time in Florida (there's no diplomatic agreement with her country that could send her home to serve jail time). Her identity will be revealed with a conviction, exposing her. She fears her family will disown her. The other inmates and guards will give her a doubly hard time for being a princess. She needs a kick-ass lawyer to straighten it all out.

Neither of us has the money for a lawyer. She spent it all on the apartment building, and I can't sell the building or even get a line of credit because the deed transfer may not be valid. It wasn't her legal name on the deed. That building mess is on hold until the trial too. If I do get the building back with a primo lawyer's help, it would be such a relief knowing I could pay for my foster dad's care. It's been a struggle on my hairdresser's salary.

So here I am, claiming her inheritance to pay a shark lawyer to save the princess. (She has to stay in Florida while waiting for her trial; otherwise, she could've just gotten the inheritance herself.) I'm practically a knight-ess in shining armor.

Only it's not all that glam. Polly kept a stiff upper lip, but she was clearly scared. If I fail, she's only got a public defender for her trial. She'll likely be convicted and suffer through a whole year of prison, a life she's completely unprepared for after being so sheltered. She's not tough like me. I learned from an early age to fight to keep what's mine and how to defend myself from the scary-ass girls I lived with in foster homes. I fear it'll break her.

Failing at my mission is no picnic for me either. If I get caught impersonating a princess, I'll be wearing orange in a cinder-block cell faster than you can say fraud. I have too many people depending on me back home to let that happen.

I take in the two-story white marble entrance hall of Amalie Palace, with its gilded mirrors and silk damask wallpaper the color of the sea with gold-leaf pattern, and try not to gawk. I'm sure it gets more luxurious the further you get into the palace. Despite the risk, I'm actually excited to get the whole royal experience. It's so far from my reality I imagine it'll be pure bliss—the best, most luxurious of everything all set at my feet. A fairy-tale life. Magical.

Butler Phillip is speaking in a gruff and growly voice to some of the servants, gesturing like he's giving orders. He's the only one in a tux, which is how I knew he was the butler. Hey, I've seen enough BBC shows to recognize a butler. Plus he spoke very proper English with a slight lilt, maybe hints of French to it, which makes sense because Villroy Island is a two-hour ferry ride from south-western France. The other servants wear white shirts with black pants. I guess Phillip is the boss man.

I give Phillip a once-over and conclude he's too perfect. He's six feet and change with wide shoulders, a barrel chest, narrow waist and hips wrapped in a tux custom fit to his frame. His eyes are a stunning aquamarine blue, sharp high cheekbones with hollows under them like you see on male models in cologne ads, five-o'clock shadow on a square jaw, and full lips. Add in his stiff formal posture and dour expression and it's no wonder I was flustered. Something is off between the butler thing and the hot thing. Not that he's my type. I like men from the real world who are fun. Like me.

A servant approaches, a thin man in his fifties with a neat comb-over. "Your Highness, I've been instructed to see you to your room."

A small snort escapes at the *Your Highness*, and then I remember I'm supposed to be a princess. "Please call me Polly. What's your name?"

"William, ma'am."

"Nice to meet you, William. Just give me a minute." I grab my wheeled suitcase from where I left it by the palace doors, turn, and nearly run into William. He reaches for my suitcase handle, and I jerk it toward me. "I can do it myself."

He holds out a palm. "If I may, ma'am? I am here to serve."

The butler stares from across the entrance hall, watching my every move. *Is he judging me? Does he suspect I'm an imposter princess?* I probably should've gotten more of a princess tutorial before arriving, but the real Polly was so stressed all she gave me was an urgent plea to get the inheritance as quickly as possible and hightail it back to Florida. "Dress in your best outfits and smile demurely" was the extent of her advice. Oh, and always call the king and queen Your Majesty; everyone else is Your Highness.

I wiggle my fingers at the dour butler and give him what I hope is a demure smile, turning my head slightly away, though I can't manage to break eye contact because his eyes have me in their judgey tractor beam.

He turns away.

Okay…I guess demure is tough to pull off.

I turn to William, who's still waiting patiently for permission to take my suitcase. "Thank you."

He inclines his head and takes the suitcase.

I follow behind him through the entrance hall, turning the corner to a long hallway. I throw a last glance over my shoulder at Phillip in profile.

He rakes a hand through his thick hair, his expression grim. He seems overwhelmed, probably because he was so surprised by my arrival.

I stop walking and hurry back to reassure him. "Relax, Butler Phillip. You won't even know I'm here."

His expression remains grim, his voice gruff and tired. "I sincerely doubt that."

I give his arm a reassuring squeeze and meet granite. He's that tense. And muscled. *What exactly do butlers do to get this buff? Powerlifting the throne for dusting? Maybe he lifts the royal dining room table with one hand while he vacuums under it.* I stifle a laugh at the thought. "Try to sneak in a nap. It'll make all the difference in the world."

He stares at my hand on his arm and then lifts his head. His aquamarine eyes are glittering and hard.

I gulp, my heart pounding. I can't help it. He's incredibly intimidating. Like I'm a hair's breadth away from bolting kind of intimidating. And I'm no shrinking violet. *I thought servants were supposed to be more…deferential or something.*

I drop my hand and try again. "Anything I can do to make things easier on you, let me know. I'm very handy."

Butler Phillip's lip curls. "Royals don't serve staff. I am here for your needs."

I smile demurely at him, just a small lift of the lips. I should probably practice in the mirror to make sure I'm not looking psycho. Or constipated. "Of course. Thank you, Phillip, and have a good day."

He looks down his nose at me.

A flare of annoyance has me lifting my chin. I'd heard butlers could be a little stuffy, but that was just rude.

"Wow." I shake my head and walk at a sedate pace in my leopard-print pumps (a rare splurge, shoes are my weakness). William is waiting for me in the long-ass hallway. Even their hallways are grand—tall frosted windows, white wood paneling, and the ceiling features gorgeous paintings with intricate plaster frames.

I'm about to ask William how old Amalie Palace is when I hear a roar of male laughter break out in the entrance hall. I turn, drawn by the fun, and see Butler Phillip stalking off in the opposite direction.

Poor guy needs to get laid.

I turn demurely back to my journey to live the royal life. For a short time anyway.

2

Gabriel

I stalk to my parents' suite of rooms in the west wing, giving up on sleep. On top of the wedding travesty and my worry over the future of the kingdom, now I have to deal with potential brides showing up at the palace door. I may never sleep again.

The servants had a good laugh over Polly actually believing I'm the butler. I grumble to myself over impertinent women wearing skintight dresses and long legs meant to wrap around…fuck. It's been too long if that brash woman is appealing to me. I blame it on sleep deprivation. I should set her straight, but I have more pressing matters. Like what my mother is up to with this bizarre plan to draw in bridal candidates with the promise of a small inheritance. Surely this will only attract the most money-hungry desperate nobility. Bottom rung for the heir. Fucking hell.

My steps slow as I approach their suite. My father is not well, late-stage pancreatic cancer, and it's painful to see him becoming weaker by the day. He's only fifty-four and used to be larger than life—vital, powerful, a proud king. Now with this damn disease, he's wasting away. My mother has been under a strain, rarely leaving his side. Theirs was an arranged marriage that turned to love, a powerful union. She doesn't want to rule without him. I worry what will become of her without her anchor.

I take a deep breath and knock. My mother's longtime maid answers the door, bowing her head as she does a deep curtsy. "Your Highness, the king is sleeping. Please let me show you to your mother's sitting room."

"Thank you, Joan."

I follow her to my mother's sitting room done in shades of pale blue with floor-to-ceiling windows offering a view of the sea she loves so much. My mother, Queen Alexandra, is seated at a small mahogany table by the window. Her dark brown hair is in a chignon, her hazel eyes sharp, her skin pale. I don't think she's spent any time outdoors in months. Her expression remains strained from her constant vigil at my father's side. We share the same hair color, same sharp cheekbones, and straight nose. My blue-green eyes are from my father. According to him, the sea color of our eyes shows we were meant to rule on this pretty island. As do our bloodlines tracing back to the original Viking tribe with their Irish wives.

The table is already set for tea for two as if she was expecting me. The servants would've passed along the message quickly of our visitor, probably gave her all the details on Polly too.

She smiles up at me, a crafty smile that doesn't quite reach her eyes. She has secrets, I can tell.

"Mother." I lean down to kiss her soft cheek.

She gestures to the chair across from her. "Have a seat, Gabriel. Would you like some tea?"

"No, thank you." I sink heavily to the cushioned chair. "I had just declared the palace closed to visitors when your guest arrived."

She takes a sip of tea, hiding her smile.

I lean forward and lower my voice. "Obviously the small inheritance she thinks she's getting is becoming my bride and inheriting Villroy. Why not just do it the traditional way quietly through royal channels?"

"What fun would that be?"

I stiffen in shock. "Fun?" My parents have drilled duty and obligation into me since birth. At no time was fun ever on the agenda.

She sighs and quietly asks the servants to give us privacy. I wait, a sense of foreboding pressing down on me.

"Your father is doing worse," she says once we're alone.

I swallow down the lump in my throat.

She blinks back tears. Emotions are private, and she keeps hers on a tight leash. "I haven't left the palace besides hospital visits in more than a year. Your bride is too important to leave it to the usual way. Gabriel, you will be king soon." Her voice catches and she takes a sip of tea. "Your wife will be queen, and the future of our kingdom depends on your mutual leadership."

I suspected as much. I hate that it's come to this, but I understand the urgency of the situation as well as my parents' need to have peace of mind that the succession will go smoothly. I only wish she would've allowed me a say in the screening process. I want a woman who brings class, dignity, and a sense of propriety to the role of queen. Not a brash impertinent rude woman in cheetah heels. Jesus.

I press my lips together, stifling my complaint over my mother's first inappropriate selection. *Please tell me there are better options heading my way.*

I steeple my fingers together on the table. "How many candidates did you invite?"

She brightens. "There are ten eligible single royals."

"And what will you do with them?" I'm thinking some kind of god-awful reception or royal ball, either of which sounds tedious as hell.

"*We* will put them to the test."

I shift in my seat, not liking the sound of this. "How?"

She looks out the window for a moment before turning back to me. "We need fresh blood, fresh ideas to help Villroy thrive again for generations to come. So we will see who is best up to the task."

"And then I will choose one?"

Her hazel eyes gleam. "The last survivor will be the one."

I jolt. She couldn't possibly mean...I lean close and whisper, "Survivor as in a battle to the death?" I know we have Viking blood, but we've been the height of royal decorum for centuries.

She rolls her eyes. "It will be like *Survivor*, that reality TV show. Your father and I have been watching a lot of TV since he's been bedridden."

My jaw drops. She's cracked under the strain of my father's illness.

She goes on in an animated voice. "There will be a series of challenges designed to eliminate those candidates not up to the task." She cocks her head. "Or maybe it will be more like that show *The Bachelor*, where we'll narrow it down by compatibility."

My gut churns as I picture women clawing their way

through whatever barbaric challenges my mother has concocted, desperate to win. Only the most aggressive woman could make it through all that, and then I will have to marry her. I need a helpmate, not a hellion.

I open my mouth to protest, but then she smiles, the first genuine smile I've seen from her in a very long time, and I nearly smile back to see it. If I wasn't being bandied about as a prize in this insane competition, I might manage it.

"Let's call it both!" she exclaims cheerfully. "*Survivor* meets *The Bachelor* royal style!"

I have to ask. "Are you feeling okay? Have you been sleeping?"

"I'm fine. I've already told your father, and he is all for it. He says it'll bring some life into the palace, and besides, this will help prepare you to be king. You'll need to use grace, diplomacy, and keen judgment to make the right choice."

This never would've happened before my father was ill. I cling to the only thin thread of reason left to me. "So it is my choice. Ultimately."

"Subject to royal approval." Which means the king and queen must also agree with my choice. King and queen trumps prince. Hell. What if I end up with the wildly inappropriate cheetah-heeled Polly as my queen because she resembles some reality TV contestant my parents like? This is madness.

I'd like to howl my displeasure, but I take one look at her rare beaming smile, and I cave. "So be it."

She squeezes my hand, a rare display of affection. "I knew you'd understand. The other women will be arriving shortly. The games begin tomorrow."

I don't even want to know. Lack of sleep, this insane

competition, my father's declining health, the future of the kingdom—my brain shuts down in protest.

I politely take my leave and make my way to my third-floor suite without a thought in my head besides sleep.

I dream of a cheetah heel clocking me on the jaw, her ankle propped on my shoulder, her body shuddering around me.

I wake in a cold sweat.

3

____

Anna

I have a maid! Her name is Anna, which freaks me out because that's my name too. I fear they're onto me, but Anna is so calm and eager to please, I'm forced to conclude I'm being paranoid. As it turns out, that's the least of my concerns because now Anna is walking me to the audience chamber in the west wing to meet Queen Alexandra for the first time about the inheritance. The queen! I'm sure I'm supposed to bow my head and curtsy. Beyond that, I'm at a loss.

I smooth clammy hands down my dress, the last of my tropical wardrobe selections. Polly is from the tropical Beaumont Islands in the Caribbean. The dress is fuchsia with a bright white and yellow flower pattern, halter top, cinched at the waist, ending mid-thigh. Too bad Polly didn't bring her royal clothes with her to Tampa or I might've matched her better. She'd shopped at Target for her new princess-in-hiding identity.

The only good news in this screwed-up situation is that Polly wore hats with veils when she was in the public eye (as required of single royal women in her homeland), so I could pass for her. We're both curly-haired brunettes, both early twenties (I'm twenty-three), similar average figure, and nearly the same height (I'm five feet nine). Polly assured me she'd never met the Villroy royalty. Her social circle was stiflingly small.

Anna gives me a tight smile as we approach the double doors of the audience chamber, which makes me nervous like she's worried for me. Maybe it's because she urged me to wear a white shawl over my shoulders and I declined. Too granny for my tastes. She also wanted to do my hair up, but who's the certified hairdresser here? I left my hair down; my curls are impossible to tame. The only thing to do with it is prevent frizz.

Not to brag, but I did put myself through beauty school and worked my way into a ritzy salon with a butt-load of happy clients. My plan has always been to scrape together enough funds to buy the salon from my boss when she retires in seven years. Owner of my own salon by thirty. I'm a big believer in manifesting your own destiny. I've got a vision board and goal Post-its all over my studio apartment. I repeat my goal like a mantra the moment I wake up: *I will own my own salon by thirty.* Some might say it's a little woo-woo. I say screw you, what can it hurt?

And didn't my destiny manifest in the form of a princess offering me a gift that could make my dream come true? Sort of. Polly and I have got a ways to go on that.

I take one step into the ornate audience chamber, nearly seize in shock, and turn to Anna. She's already out the door, which shuts neatly behind her. I turn back and take a deep calming breath. The massive room makes me feel small—gold trim on everything, a ceiling that looks like it dates back to the Renaissance with elaborate paintings of ethereal beings, an enormous crystal chandelier shining over glossy inlaid hardwood floors. Scores of royal ancestors look down their noses at me from oil paintings along the walls, and at the very end of this massively intimidating room is a huge antique wooden double throne. Queen Alexandra sits there, alone, in a powder blue long-sleeved dress with matching heels, pearl necklace, pearl earrings. She is the definition of regal class, and I'm suddenly feeling like I should've worn something less tropical and more in the pastel family.

As if that isn't intimidating enough, nine women flank the throne in a sea of pastels and straight glossy hair, standing in two neat arcs like a royal beauty pageant is about to take place. My only chance is Miss Congeniality.

I seriously consider bolting. My wild curls and tropical dress stick out like a giraffe at a petting zoo. Before I can make my escape, a servant is at my side, urging me to take my place with the other women. Is Polly's small inheritance to be split ten ways? Because I don't think that's going to cut it for lawyer's fees.

I'm nearly at the end of the line on the left when a man in a crisp white shirt and black pants announces, "Princess Mary Louise Lyon of the Beaumont Islands."

I gulp. That's me. My pulse pounding in my ears, I pray I don't screw this up for her. I take three steps forward, bow my head to the queen, and do a deep curtsy. I'm not sure how long to hold it. Three seconds seems right. I slowly straighten and address her directly, "Pleased to meet you, Your Majesty."

The queen smiles, a gentle smile. "Thank you for traveling all this way, Mary. Please join the others."

I comply, sensing some serious side-eye from the other women.

The queen addresses us and drops a bombshell. "I've asked you all here on false pretenses."

A shocked silence falls. Crap. No inheritance?

The queen continues. "You're not here to claim a small inheritance." She pauses, and the tension is so thick it makes me want to shout *Go on!* Finally, she does. "You are here for riches beyond your dreams. However, only one of you will be granted these riches."

The women murmur quietly to each other.

The queen doesn't elaborate further. Welp, somebody has to ask.

I raise my hand. "How do you decide who gets it?"

The queen's eyes narrow, her lips pressed tightly together.

"Your Majesty," I add belatedly.

The queen addresses the room in a crisp tone. "Before we go further, I must ask you to sign a nondisclosure." She gestures toward a small table, where a man in a charcoal gray suit is waiting to witness the signings. "If you choose not to, you may leave now."

Not one person leaves. We form an obedient line, because who doesn't need riches beyond their dreams? Though I suspect some of us might need those riches more than others. I have to hand those riches over to Polly, but she assured me a portion would go toward my foster dad, Mike's care.

I cleared my schedule and took two weeks' vacation time to make this happen. You know when the last time was that I took a vacation? Uh, never. My goal always in mind—own my own salon by thirty—means I always work. Even at home, I'm on call for whatever a tenant might need. I'm the super for our apartment building and live rent-free because of it. I can fix lots of stuff thanks to Mike, who was a handyman. I don't mind hard work. It gets me where I want to go.

I'm last to sign, and I take the time to read the fine print. No talking to the press, no photos, no social media, cell phones to be turned in for the duration. Hey! No phone? What kind of retro technophobic place is this? Can I live without my phone? Who will be there to watch the cat videos? It's my stress reliever. I'm tense just thinking about not having my phone. I keep reading the fine print for more red flags. We're required to commit to three weeks for the competition. Three weeks? Competition?

The time frame is going to be tough. I think I can survive without my phone if I'm busy winning this competition, whatever it is. I could probably beat the demure princess squad at most anything. They're wispy, overly polite women used to being waited on, not used to going after what they want like me. But it's cutting it really close to Polly's court date, which is only a week after the competition ends. And if I don't win the big prize here, that extra week of unpaid days is going to hurt. Mike's care immediately comes to mind. The doctors say there's nothing more that can be done for him, and they sent him home to die. Lung cancer. My throat tightens, as it does every time I think of him dying. His foster home was the last one I landed in at seventeen. He even let me stay rent-free in the studio apartment over his garage after I aged out of the foster system. I couldn't have put myself through beauty school without that safe place to land. I only wish we'd found each other sooner.

I force my mind to practicalities. I'll dip into my meager savings to cover Mike's nurse this month. He deserves that much. My boss at the salon is super cool and wants me to be the future owner of her salon, so that's in my favor, but I'm not sure if she'll be okay with me not being there for so long. My clients are some of the wealthiest, and they're very attached to me. The relationship with your hairdresser is sacred. And who will do my job at the apartment building dealing with the tenants? What if I end up homeless and unemployed? My savings won't cover me and a home nurse for very long.

I glance around at the sea of pastel princesses, which reminds me of Polly, who probably used to exclusively wear pastels and pearls and is now facing wearing orange and getting beat up on the regular by some tough bitch named Spike. I don't know the bitch's name, but I bet I'm close.

I raise my hand, glancing at the queen on her throne and then the lawyer guy across the table from me, making sure they both hear me. "I have a question. What competition could possibly take three weeks?"

Silence. The princesses dart dark looks at me. *What? I'm the only one who cares about the specifics?*

"I mean, I only get two weeks…" I trail off, suddenly realizing Polly doesn't have a job with specific vacation-time restrictions. "I have some prior commitments."

"Change them," the queen says as if she fully expects to be obeyed.

I worry my lower lip. If I can't work it out with my boss back home, this might be over before it even begins.

The lawyer guy speaks up. "Only the winner will remain for the full three weeks. It's entirely possible you won't make it that long." His lip curls like he expects me to lose whatever this thing is right away.

I square my shoulders and straighten my spine. I have

never backed down from a challenge. I'll get a friend to apartment-sit, have her farm out any emergency repair work for the tenants, and hold the small things for my return. I'll beg my boss at the salon for the time off and convince my clients to wait for me by offering a free home styling for any special occasion. I will emerge victorious. That's my new mantra—victory! For Polly, for me, for Mike, and to shove it in this snotty lawyer's face.

Besides, riches beyond our dreams should take care of everything. Polly wouldn't let me wallow in debt after saving her ass. Of course, that's only if I win. It's still a huge risk I'm taking personally and professionally. Not to mention the risk of getting caught impersonating a princess. Harsh reality hits at the thought, and I suddenly can't get a deep breath. At best, I end up in prison back home, destroying my reputation and my plan to own my own salon, unable to afford Mike's nurse. Clients have to trust you. Convicted felons do not inspire confidence.

Or I could be held accountable for my crime right here on Villroy Island. This monarchy has real power. As in, their island, their rules. I couldn't find any recent executions in my brief internet search, but I'm well aware that, if caught, my chances of quietly slipping away from an island accessible only by boat are slim. It's a two-hour ferry ride to France over choppy sea, and even I'm not that strong a swimmer. These royals might be so pissed off they'll roll out an old rusty guillotine or, worse, throw me in a dungeon with spiders. *Shudder.* (It's a phobia. Doesn't mean I'm not tough.)

Plus, if I'm caught, that means the real Polly will be exposed under a storm of bad publicity. People will want her to pay for her crime. Her family will disown her. She'll lose everything.

I suck in air, my gut churning. No room for self-doubt. Think of Polly—bright and cheerful Polly—so happy to experience freedom for the first time in her life. She deserves that.

Victory, victory, victory.

I manage a deep breath in and out. *Focus. Get the inheritance; get out.*

I pull it together and turn to the queen. "Any wiggle room on the no-phone policy?"

The queen stares at me.

The lawyer guy answers in a vaguely threatening tone like he's *this close* to strangling me. "You may use the palace phone in the parlor if absolutely necessary."

The pieces settle into place in my mind in an alarming way. We're on an island, isolated from the outside world both geographically and communication-wise, and the nature of this competition has still not been revealed. My mind flashes to every creepy horror movie I've ever seen. Lawyer guy saying "you won't make it that long" suddenly sounds ominous. I glance around at the other women, but nobody seems to be getting it. We're being isolated, tested, and maybe dispatched too!

"What's going on here?" I holler.

And then the queen herself approaches, drawing a collective gasp as she crosses the room to face me across the small table.

We lock eyes, and I belatedly remember I'm supposed to be demure, curtsy and all that shit, but I'm spooked, and it's just not possible. What have I gotten myself into? My brain screams *Polly needs you,* and my gut screams *these people are crazy; get out while you can!* I'm sure I'd be the first to die in a horror movie. I'd just be standing there, frozen, while the hatchet came down, and everyone in the audience screamed, "Run!"

The queen speaks quietly as if she senses my freak-out. "You are not like the others."

Shit. I was too much me. I scramble for a suitable princess-type response in as calm a voice as I can manage. "We do things differently on Beaumont. Everyone is too hot to be anything but relaxed due to the tropical climate." I plaster on a smile and immediately tone it down, trying for a slight curve of the lips, a demure smile that feels like maybe I'm pursing my lips a little in a fish face. Not royally appropriate. Gah! "Your Majesty," I add.

She inclines her head regally. "Would you like to decline?"

"What do you plan to do with the contestants who don't win?" I whisper.

"You'll return to your kingdom, much richer for the experience."

The *richer* reminds me of my true purpose here, funds for Polly's fancy lawyer. I need to gird my loins and be her knight-ess in shining armor.

I meet Queen Alexandra's hazel eyes, and they're gleaming with unholy delight like she's got something devious up her sleeve. "I'll work something out, Your Majesty. May I ask exactly what the competition entails?"

The queen whispers, "Have you seen *Survivor*?"

My eyes widen. Never in a zillion years would I have thought she'd ask that. I calm down because at least we're out of horror-movie territory. If this is some kind of primal nature challenge, I'm not exactly trained for that, but my survival instincts are sharp. Had to be where I come from. I'm tough and strong.

"I'm in." Anna Hebert is about to trounce the competition. I mean, Polly Lyon. I sign her name with a flourish.

"Excellent," the queen pronounces before returning to her throne with a little bounce in her step.

Pleased that the queen seems pleased, I return to my place with the women, all of us waiting for our next instruction.

The queen lifts a hand. "Please make whatever arrangements you need, and then hand over your phones to Albert." She indicates an older stooped man with thinning white hair in the servant's uniform of white shirt with black pants. "The competition will begin on Point Beach at noon."

"What should I wear?" I ask.

The room falls silent. The other women stare at me like I'm an odd duck. Or giraffe, as the case may be. I'm definitely not blending, but am I really the only one with questions?

"Wear whatever is suitable for fishing," the queen pronounces.

This causes a demure uproar among the women, none of them directly addressing the queen. Subdued outrage is probably the best description. I've never fished, but hey! I'm from Tampa and used to the water. I'm a strong swimmer. And I brought my bikini. All set. I'm feeling a little smug about the way things are playing out when a man in a navy pin-striped suit strides in like he owns the place. It's Butler Phillip. He's not wearing the butler tux for some reason. Maybe he's off duty. His expression is just as grim and dour as I remember. The hollows under his cheekbones are more pronounced when his jaw is tight like now. Maybe he's here to set up the competition stuff.

He continues walking straight to the queen. He must

be sure of his place with the royal family because he bends to kiss her cheek and then faces us.

The women are eerily silent.

And then I see it—the similarities between Butler Phillip and the queen, same dark brown hair, same sharp cheekbones, though Phillip has striking aquamarine eyes and the queen's eyes are hazel. This must be her son. Which would mean…holy royal fuckup!

The queen lifts a palm, gesturing toward him without being so rude as to point. "Crown Prince Gabriel will judge the competition with me. Good luck to you all!"

I send the imposter butler my best death glare. Why did he let me think he was a servant? Have I completely screwed up this thing for Polly? The way I spoke to him! I nearly cringe when my words come back to me. After he told me his name was Butler Phillip, I said: *Just like Prince Phillip, the royal hottie! Much cooler than the heir to the throne. That guy, oh, man, I heard he's a dud.*

I called the crown prince of Villroy a dud! And he's the judge of this competition!

Worse, I said he was a real stick-in-the-mud *and* he needed to get over himself. Phillip is his brother. Obviously he was messing with me. Do haughty crown princes mess with princesses? Wait, he said he was Butler Phillip before I told him I had royal blood. What is his deal? He gets off on pretending to be a servant?

His haughty gaze rakes me from head to toe, and then he lifts one arrogant brow. That brow says *ha-ha, now you know. Grovel before me.*

I lift my chin. I don't grovel.

One corner of his mouth lifts in a sexy smirk that enrages me. He's enjoying his high horse.

I take a step forward, about to give him a piece of my

mind when I remember I'm supposed to be pastel and pearl demure. I have a quick internal battle over how I can ream him without risking my cover. But then the queen says something to him, and he frowns. They both leave without a backward glance.

The princesses clear out too.

I rush back to my room to make arrangements back home. I can't let my fear of future unemployed homelessness and spider-infested dungeons cloud my thinking. I must remain focused to win. And to show up Prince Gabriel the imposter butler!

4

___

I take one step onto the beach in my leopard-print bikini and freeze, mortified by my complete miscalculation. No one is wearing a bikini, not even a one-piece. My cheeks burn as, one by one, the princesses turn to check me out.

Much tittering and whispering ensues. The other women are wearing capris, Bermuda shorts, fussy short-sleeved blouses with cap sleeves, tiny pearl buttons, ruffles and shit.

Giraffe meet petting zoo.

I force my legs to keep moving forward despite the whispers, despite the queen's disapproving look, despite the beefy security guards flanking the queen, who I'm sure are checking me out through their shades. It's not like I have time to run all the way back to the palace, change, and get back in time for the competition. I stifle a sigh. It's a sunny June day, probably in the eighties. It's like princesses don't do casual. They don't show much skin either. Everything is buttoned up to the neck, nothing sleeveless. I suddenly know why Anna was pushing the shawl on me earlier. There must be some kind of royal rule about not showing bare shoulders or boobage or something.

Whatever. I'm here to win.

I plant myself near the group, reach up to the clear blue sky, and stretch. Then I shake out my legs. I take solace in the fact that the leopard is my spirit animal, which is why it's so heavily represented in my wardrobe. Leopards are strong, bold, and persistent.

I figure we must be doing this fishing thing the old-fashioned way because the only things on the beach—besides the other princesses and the queen with her security guards—are nets and large baskets. We'll probably be swimming out to some fishing area and scooping up as many fish as we can with our nets. I'm not squeamish. I got this.

The queen is wearing her same dress with flats. Her four guards are in black T-shirts with black pants. These guys are stone-cold serious. Makes me want to flash them to see if I can make them break.

I approach one of the women, a princess who looks like an angel—her blond hair in a neat bun, big blue eyes, pert little nose. She's standing apart from the herd. Maybe she doesn't know the other women either. Maybe we could be friends or allies. "Hi, I'm Polly."

She smiles demurely and really pulls it off. "I'm Marguerite."

"Where are you from?"

"Alvilda."

I've never heard of it, but Polly probably has. "Does Alvilda need riches?"

Her voice is soft and melodic. "Every kingdom must protect its legacy by any means necessary."

"Yeah, but isn't this a little crazy? A competition among royals? We're above this kind of thing."

She licks her lips, staring at the new arrival. Gabriel. The blood rushes through my veins because for once he doesn't look too perfect. In fact, he looks almost normal in a gray T-shirt with black athletic shorts. His regal stance, proud and powerful, gives him away though. What I thought was a stuffy butler proud of his place in the household was actually a prince groomed to be king. Aviator shades hide his expression, though his jaw still looks tight, his full lips pressed together. The queen must really be taking this competition seriously to involve Gabriel. Where's the king? Is something wrong with him? And why are they giving away riches? Is something wrong with Villroy itself? How am I the only one with questions? Did all of these princesses have curiosity drilled out of them with their etiquette lessons? *Smile demurely, go along, follow the protocol.* No wonder the real Polly went in hiding to Florida to live a little.

Another man arrives—a servant, I can tell by his white shirt and black pants uniform—carrying a large box. I've yet to meet the real butler. I hope he's in a tux or at least a suit. I'm still hoping for the royal experience. The butler's name should be Jeeves or Nigel, no, Edwin.

The servant dumps the contents of the box upside down onto the sand. It's a large inflatable raft, all folded up. No air compressor, not even a manual pump.

We all stare at the raft.

The queen pipes up. "You'll work together to inflate the raft, take it out to the inlet, and fish. The person who brings back the most fish wins. Please take a net and basket."

The women slowly make their way to the nets and baskets. Not me. I head for the raft and unfold it, hoping there's at least a manual pump tucked inside it. Nope. And I'm not so sure it can hold ten women either, even lightweights like these ladies. I get on my hands and knees and search the whole damn thing for a self-inflate trigger and, finding none, open up the valve and puff a few breaths into it. Barely a lift.

I look up from where I'm still kneeling on the sand to find Gabriel staring at me. I can feel it even through the aviator shades. "Is there an air pump somewhere?"

He gestures toward the queen.

I stand and ask the queen the same question, remembering to add Your Majesty. She bestows a small *Mona Lisa* smile on me, which is not an answer.

I head over to the nets and baskets, snagging the last one of each. Oh, great, my net is torn. The goal is the most fish, not the biggest, so I'd figured on catching a lot of little fish. Now they'll fall right out of the net. I quickly knot the frayed sides together. The tear is fixed, but now my net is misshapen. What can you do? I wasted time on the raft, so I get last pickings. *You snooze, you lose.*

The queen lifts a hand. "We'll return in two hours to choose a winner. That person will have a say in the next competition. Last place will go home on the next ferry."

She leaves, security going with her; then Gabriel and the servant leave too.

Once they're out of sight, we all look at each other.

"You," a woman says imperiously, jabbing a long clear polished fingernail at me, "inflate the raft."

I narrow my eyes. "It's Polly, not *you,* and I couldn't

inflate that thing if I wanted to. It's huge. Look, they're gone. All that matters is catching fish. We'll just swim out, scoop some up, and come back to shore."

"But they said we have to take the raft to the inlet," someone whines.

"I can't swim," Marguerite says forlornly.

I blow out a breath of frustration. It seems like an impossible challenge. I look around at the dunes, the high rocky cliffs, searching for cameras. Is the real competition to see what happens in the face of the impossible? I don't see any cameras. The queen is one sick son of a bitch.

"Hurry before the tide gets high," a red-haired princess says. And then she rushes into the shallow waves, her net in the water.

The other women follow, jostling each other for space. A few get knocked down and come up sputtering. A fight breaks out, and my jaw drops, eyes wide. It's *vicious*. Lots of screaming, flying fists, and hair pulling.

Well, damn, it didn't take long for the princesses to go *Lord of the Flies* out there. My lovely royal fantasy is shattered. I shake my head. Ya know, the *one* thing I was looking forward to in this whole crazy situation was getting the royal experience. Now I know the truth. People are people, even if they're born with a silver spoon in their mouth. It's like I just found out Santa isn't real. No magic left in the world.

I let out a long sigh. I guess I'll just wait for them to stop splashing around so much, scaring the fish away. I'm willing to bet they give up soon.

~

Gabriel

Immediately following the presentation of the first challenge, I join my mother in the royal chambers, where my father lies bedridden. We've kept his health concerns quiet, but he's past the point where medicine can help him. The TV screen mounted within view of his bed features a closed-circuit view of the women on the beach.

My father is smiling. "Well done, Alexandra. Fishing is the perfect challenge. Everyone should understand how life works around here." Villroy has a long history of fishing dating back to the early Viking settlers. The original tribe of Vikings was known as the Wild Ones. I like that I'm descended from wild people. I may have squashed those rougher tendencies under royal decorum, but they're there. I'm a warrior king born in the wrong century.

Those original Vikings sailed down from an early settlement on the Irish islands, bringing their Irish wives. Later, the British took over, then the French. A couple of centuries ago, the Rourke line was reestablished from the original Viking Irish roots. Under Rourke leadership, Villroy became a major seafood supplier. Now, with declining fish populations, it's more work for less catch, and the fishermen are forced farther out to sea. The younger generation head over to mainland Europe for better opportunities. A population made up only of the older generation cannot survive as a kingdom for long. We need something to keep the younger generation here, offer them jobs and better opportunities than they could get elsewhere. This is what keeps me up at night.

My mother takes the chair next to my father's bed, stroking his hand and murmuring, "I'm glad you like it."

It hits me that she's created her own reality TV show for his benefit. Another reminder that, while my parents began their marriage as strangers, their bond is now tight. Love can make you do strange things. Normally, my parents are the height of decorum and royal grace. My father's illness has changed them both, knowing they don't have much time left together.

I have to ask. "And how will this determine the best bride for me?"

My mother turns to me. "I told you we need fresh blood with fresh ideas for the future of Villroy. These challenges are set up to find the best candidate."

My father nods, his gaze glued to the TV.

"By making them fish?" I ask, not bothering to hide my skepticism. I still think this is all for my father's entertainment. My bride's royal duties will not include fishing.

"It's tradition, Gabriel," my mother snaps.

"Yes, tradition," my father echoes.

I clench my jaw. Fishing may have been part of our ancestors' lives, but it hasn't been a regular thing for us royals in generations. "Where are the cameras?"

"Everywhere," my mother replies, her eyes glued to the screen. "Cameras nowadays are so small it's not hard at all to place them."

A horrifying thought occurs. "Even in the bedrooms? The bathrooms?"

My mother shoots me a dark look. "Please, Gabriel. You mustn't think of seducing one of them. That would completely defeat the purpose of the games."

I grind my teeth. "If there's a camera in my bedroom—"

"There isn't," my mother says. "You think I want *us* on film in our private moments? The guest bedrooms and bathrooms remain private as well."

"Don't worry," my father says. "Your mother and I

thought this out. We're like TV producers. It was all in the nondisclosure they signed."

"We're directors too," my mother says proudly.

I stifle a groan. When in the nuthouse, do as the nuts do. I return my attention to the screen. The women are splashing in the shallows; the waves are mild at low tide. They're swinging their fishing nets around wildly, except Polly, who is busy folding up the raft. In her bikini. The round firm globes of her ass point up as she bends to her task. I want to take a bite. *Not her.* She is the antithesis of what a queen should be—ill-mannered, loud, barely wearing anything. Why must she fold the raft? Why is she wearing a bikini? She should be covered like the other women. I spare a glance at the other princesses, and even from this distance, it's like a wet T-shirt contest, their clothes transparent. My eyes dart back to Polly.

"That one stands out, doesn't she?" my mother asks. "I like her."

"She comes from an island kingdom, which is a plus," my father puts in.

My eyes are glued to her luscious body. "You mean Polly?" My voice comes out rough.

"Oh, no, not her!" my mother exclaims. "She'd never do as queen. She's made no effort to blend in with the other women. She's too much on the outside, and her accent is ghastly. Clearly she wasn't raised in her homeland."

Her accent is American—unrefined, bold, and brash. Exactly like her. I shouldn't like it, but I do. It makes me think she'd be bold in other ways. The kind of woman who'd satisfy me.

"Her accent can be tamed, my dear," my father says and then breaks off in a long coughing fit. My mother urges him to sip from a nearby glass of water. Once he settles down, he goes on, "Our sources told us she is something of a rough diamond, but we agreed that the fact that she comes from a prosperous island makes for a useful alliance." He turns to me. "Gabriel's influence will bring her to heel."

Nothing will bring that woman to heel. I incline my head, keeping my opinion to myself because I don't mind Polly being around for a bit if she's going to keep wearing sexy clothes. And bikinis.

My father turns back to my mother and says in a teasing voice, "You had quite the accent once." My mother is from a small kingdom off the coast of Australia. Her accent, after working with a dialect coach, is now nearly gone. In its place is proper English with a slight French lilt similar to Villroy's accent. Many of the islanders of today are from France since Villroy is off the coast of France. English is the official language, though many are bilingual.

My mother shakes her head at my father, like Polly's accent is a lost cause, before turning to me. "I meant Marguerite, the petite blond, stands out. Did you see her toss the redhead on her ass?"

My jaw drops. The queen does not say *ass*. I snap my mouth shut, at a loss for how to talk to this version of the queen mother.

"The redhead is Elizabeth," my father says. He points a knobby finger at the screen. He's lost so much weight. "Polly reminds me of my brother's scrappy wife." His voice is hoarse, and he takes a sip of water. "All their rough lot. Have you heard from my brother?"

My ears perk at this. My father must be in worse shape than I thought to be asking for his older brother. After all the bad blood, I doubt he'll hear back. My father and his brother haven't been in touch since my uncle abdicated the throne to marry a commoner—an American from Brooklyn, New York. It was a huge scandal at the time. Never been done in the history of the kingdom. My father was furious he had to give up his dream of becoming a professional football player. He'd just been recruited to France's team after graduating university. From what I hear, my father was living the high life while his brother did his duty. It was a harsh change.

"Not yet," my mother murmurs.

My uncle was cast out after he married his wife. My cousins are often referred to as the riffraff despite being half royal. Their family is not welcome in Villroy and remains in Brooklyn. My youngest sister, Silvia, had connected with them while studying at university in the US and reported back to us that they were a gruff lot. Six brothers. Maybe they could've been less gruff with my baby sister? Silvia is such a bleeding heart, she didn't mind. She's still trying to mend fences that can never be mended. Probably she's softened in her time in the US, especially after marrying an American. It wasn't a big deal for her to marry a commoner since she was seventh in line for the throne. For the oldest, me, it matters. I've been groomed to carry on the legacy and I will. My wife will be a true queen. In the meantime…

I resume watching Polly's shapely ass as she works to fold up the raft. Why is she straightening up the beach when she's supposed to be fishing? Finally, she finishes the task and sits on top of the folded raft, watching the women splashing around in the water. The fish have probably been scared away.

The Polly Show now over, I take my leave.

My parents barely notice.

Anna

I'm sitting on the folded-up raft, watching the women's wrestling show in the water with a mixture of horror and fascination as the claws and teeth come out. Someone screams as her hair is pulled. So much hair pulling. Scratching, biting, slapping, and kicking too. It's brutal. Someone rips a shirt, the buttons pinging off into the water.

"Anyone catch anything?" I call during a pause in the action.

The red-haired princess holds up her net triumphantly and there's a small silver fish wriggling in there. Marguerite snatches the net from her and tosses her an empty net in return.

"You bitch!" Red Hair screeches.

The two go down swinging into the shallow water. Hopefully nobody drowns; otherwise I'll have to do CPR. I'm all Red Cross certified from my previous job as a lifeguard. I keep it up. You never know when it'll come in handy.

I wiggle my feet deeper into the sand and feel something hard, much bigger than a shell. I kneel down and dig around a bit. A treasure! I pull out a box containing an air pump, the kind you pump with your foot. The servant dropped the raft right over it. They must've thought we'd stumble upon it as we worked together to get this raft thing going. I hook the tube into the valve and start pumping. "You guys! I got the air pump. It'll be easier to fish if we can take it out to the inlet. Dig around in the sand; maybe there's some paddles too."

There's a brief pause in the action before the women go back to their fierce, clumsy battle for fish.

I keep pumping. It's a pretty good pump and inflates the raft faster than I thought it would. An hour later, I'm drenched in sweat, my legs are burning from the workout of pumping this thing, but I've got the raft fully inflated. I'm too tired to dig around in the sand for paddles, if there even are any. The women are scattered around, some of them still trying for fish, a few just sitting in the shallow water, their nets out in case a fish happens to swim in. A few of the princesses are floating on their backs past the waves.

I toss my net and basket into the raft and drag it to the water. "Hop in. I'll bet there's lots of fish over by the inlet. We'll paddle with our hands." I hold it steady as everyone clambers in, some of them flopping like fish into the bottom of it. I push off and climb in with them. And it works! We're paddling with our hands and moving in the right direction.

We make it to the inlet, a sheltered spot of sea between some rocky cliffs. I can see the fish just below the surface. Jackpot!

The princesses must be tired because they sit listlessly, their nets in the water. I'm tired too from all that pumping action, but I need to catch up. The most that's been caught by a princess are three little fish. All I have to do is beat three.

I lean over, looking for a school of fish, hoping to scoop them in one swish, when someone knocks me into the water. "Ahhh!"

I bob to the surface and shove my mop of curls out of

my face. "What the hell? After I pumped that raft for you all? Who pushed me?"

The women stare at me. They look like savages, a bedraggled grim lot with their clothes soaked through, their hair a mess from salt water and the previous hair pulling. Nobody fesses up.

Every survival instinct I have kicks into play. They want me off the raft? Then I'll fish from here in the water, better than they could. I hang onto the raft with one hand and fish as deep as I can reach, slowly moving my net through the water. *Come on, little fishie, swim a little closer.*

A tug alerts me I've got something. I scoop it toward the surface. Holy crap. It's big, thrashing around in my net, and I can barely hang on. Its mouth has snaggly fangs. I toss it into the raft, where it flops around. The princesses scream, rushing to get away from it. Next thing I know, half of them tip into the water, scrambling too far on the other side of the raft.

The women still in the raft cackle with glee. Nothing like competition to bring out the best in women.

I smile to myself and go back to fishing. I catch something small and leave it in there as bait.

By the time a large motorized raft pulls up to rescue—err, to call a halt to the competition—I've caught one biggie and four little fish. I climb into our much smaller raft to snag the big fish I'd tossed in earlier, but it's gone. A quick scan of the other women's baskets tells me someone tossed my big fish overboard.

A crew member helps us onto the bigger raft along with our nets and baskets. The smaller raft is tied to it for a tow. Gabriel and the queen are nowhere to be found. We're deposited back on shore, where three men wait—

two serious-as-hell security guards and the servant who gave us the raft.

The servant approaches. "Ladies, please place your baskets in front of you." He inspects the line of us, counting the fish.

Marguerite, who can't swim, who spent half her time stealing other people's fish, wins with five fish and a fish head, which shouldn't count. I underestimated her with her angelic looks. I'll have to keep a close eye on that one.

She smiles demurely, still looking angelic despite her raggedy appearance after an afternoon of sun, sand, salt water, and bitch fighting.

The losers are two women who have one fish each. They're immediately escorted away by security.

Was it a coincidence that there were two security guards dispatched for the two women eliminated? Or were we being watched the whole time?

Later that night, after we've all had a chance to wash up and refresh, we're informed we'll be joining the queen and crown prince for dinner in the royal dining room. Now this is more like it! The true royal experience is finally happening. The fact that it hasn't been so far—the princesses are savages, the queen doesn't approve of me, and the crown prince is no prince charming—does nothing to dim my hopes for a royal dinner. I'm a cock-eyed optimist, but guess what? It's gotten me this far in life, and I'm pretty happy with where I'm at.

I pull on the only dress I own that covers my shoulders, white with black polka dots, with a plunging neckline and short skirt. A gold chain belt cinches neatly at the waist. Other than asking the queen for a new wardrobe, I don't know what I'm supposed to do to fit in better. I suppose I could tuck a handkerchief or scarf into my cleavage to cover it, but that's not who I am. I'm a *what you see is what you get* kind of woman. *But Polly the princess isn't.* I borrow the demure white shawl and arrange it diagonally across me like a long scarf. Cleavage and shoulders covered. Now the question is, nude high-heeled sandals or leopard pumps? I go with the sandals.

The elegant dining room doesn't disappoint. A long gleaming dark wood table is set with china, silver, crystal, and a huge floral centerpiece. I'm quickly escorted in by a servant and offered a drink. Some of the princesses are already seated. There are small name cards. Assigned seating. I scan the names on the hunt for my own. Francesca, Elizabeth, Sophia, and Marguerite are seated closest to the queen and prince at the head of the table.

I make my way down the table to the other end and find myself at the furthest point away from the royal pair. Marguerite won the competition, so it makes sense for her to be seated closest to the queen. They probably need to discuss whatever the next challenge is. I debated speaking up about Marguerite's dirty play with the fish, but decided at this early stage in the competition, it didn't matter that much. I'm still in it, and the risk of getting on Marguerite's bad side and further irritating the queen doesn't seem wise. I'm sure the rest of the seating is random. After all, I was second place, and if it were place order, I'd be seated much closer.

I know everyone's names now, having wrung it out of them on the raft ride back to shore. I'm good with names. It helps in the salon business to quickly warm up the customers. I'm sure the real Polly would be pleased I'm connecting with them. Though I have to say she must not have had much contact with the royal world because not one person questions me stepping in for her. She must've been kept on a tight leash. Her reckless undercover adventure makes a lot more sense now. Before, I would've said, how could you give up being a princess?

A hush falls over the room as the queen enters followed by the prince. Everyone stands. My eyes are drawn to Gabriel. He's still too perfect, too haughty and arrogant, but there's simply no getting around the fact that he is gorgeous. He's in a dark blue suit custom tailored to his muscular body. I'm dying to get a look at those shoulders filling out the blazer so nicely, but doubt he'll ever appear shirtless just for my leering gaze. Royal decorum and all that. The queen looks pleased, a small smile on her face as she takes her seat at the head of the table, wearing a long-sleeved pale yellow dress. Gabriel gestures for us to take a seat and then takes his place at the queen's right.

"How nice to see you all," the queen says. "I trust you've had some time to refresh after today's outing?"

The women murmur politely. I'm dying to ask what the next challenge is because I was close to winning, and that means there's still a chance to help out poor Polly, but the servants begin serving the first course, so I keep quiet.

The food, mostly seafood, is excellent. Better than I've ever had, fresh caught from the sea. The conversation is subdued. By the time I finish my third glass of wine, I'm feeling pretty, *pretty* relaxed. I stifle a yawn. Who knew all this royal luxury could put me to sleep? Growing up, sometimes hungry after a meager meal—there never seemed to be enough food to go around at some of the foster homes—I imagined living in a royal palace would be heaven. I suppose I've been on my own for so long that being served and sitting passively instead of doing for myself is boring. My royal fantasy is dead, never to be resuscitated again. Le sigh.

I catch Gabriel's eye. Something about his rigid demeanor makes me want to make him laugh, tickle him or surprise it out of him. His laugh would probably sound rusty like he hadn't laughed in a decade or more. I'm pretty sure his teeth are ground to nubs from all the jaw clenching he does. I wink at him just to see what happens.

His lips twitch, and my stomach flutters in anticipation of his smile. The queen says something to him and he turns away. I'm ridiculously disappointed.

The queen stands, and we all rush to stand too. She gestures for us to take a seat again. "I have an announcement. Marguerite has chosen the next competition, and it will be a treasure hunt on the island. The clues are related to nature, and you'll need to do some out-of-the-box thinking to figure it out." She smiles unexpectedly. "Isn't this fun?"

The women murmur agreement.

Fun? More like insanity for your entertainment. She's probably watching us compete, like her own reality TV show from her secret royal lair.

The queen goes on in a dramatic tone, clearly enjoying herself. "I promised you riches beyond your dreams, and now I will explain. Crown Prince Gabriel is the real prize. Snag this royal catch and you will inherit the wealth of our kingdom. Provided, of course, you are the most qualified to be his bride after many more fun and challenging tasks."

My stomach drops. WTF. The riches beyond our dreams are tied to a marriage? Everything in me screams *no!*

No to giving up my life back home.

No to the rigid stick-in-the-mud.

No to a miserable soulless existence filled with duties and no fun at all. Thank God my royal fantasy was shattered earlier or I might be taken in.

All eyes turn toward Gabriel. His jaw is granite. His expression is brooding and maybe a little resigned.

The queen takes her leave, and everyone stands, murmuring polite goodbyes.

The moment she leaves the room, the women nearly knock over their chairs in their hurry to approach Gabriel. He towers above them, proud and regal. Even so, his expression is hunted. The women are all over him, a cacophony of high-pitched excitement. *Gold diggers.*

I loosen my clenched fists, surprised at the stab of jealousy. It's not like *I* want to marry him. He's rigid and haughty, part of a world that I could never fit into. Would the real Polly want to marry him? I'm not so sure. She's similar to me—bold and free-spirited—and Gabriel is so not. He's all buttoned into his rigid role, and I suspect he enjoys it in some tense weird way. On the other hand, the sleazy guy Polly's parents are pressuring her to marry only wants her for her royal connections. He's an older businessman on Beaumont, and she says he's promised her parents to have a firm hand with her. That was a red flag to both me and Polly.

Even if I won Gabriel, I'm not Polly—the truth would come out for sure with an engagement—and then Polly and I would both be finished. Maybe I should bail. This looks like a no-win situation.

But then Gabriel shoots me a desperate look from across the room, practically begging me to save him from the princess posse. It almost seems like maybe he needs me. Like he's just a regular guy trapped in circumstances beyond his control. Just like Polly.

Gah. I can't be the royal rescuer for everyone. *Man up and shake off the prissy women.* I need to figure out next steps for Polly.

I turn and head for the door. I swear I can feel Gabriel's eyes following me.

5

____

Anna

After pacing the palace halls forever, I head outside, hoping the night air will clear my head. I take off my sandals as soon as I reach the palace courtyard, feeling the cool grass between my toes. I turn and take in the palace in the moonlight. It really is like something out of a fairy tale—sandstone with copper roofs, five stories, six stories in the two towers, multiple spires. The courtyard is surrounded on both sides by the two long wings of the palace. I turn and keep walking through the courtyard, heading to the large expanse of manicured gardens. It's peaceful here, like everything is under control from the box hedges in straight lines to the perfectly shaped trees, to the four long terraces of grassy slopes leading down to the sea.

A whimsical marble fountain lit up with pink and blue lights comes into view. Up close, copper fish spout water at each other in playful arcs. I love it. I take a seat on a long wooden bench across from the fountain under a large arch of pink roses. The steady splash of water, the distant sound of waves, the scent of roses, all of it combined soothes me. I'm at a rare loss. Unsure which way to go, forward or retreat.

I exhale sharply. I can't believe I was lured to Villroy, or more accurately, Polly was lured here with the promise of a small inheritance only to be told it was "riches beyond our dreams," and then that the real prize was Gabriel. The desperate hunted look in his eyes when all those princesses rushed him makes me wonder how he feels about being the prize in this competition. Personally, I would hate being treated like a trophy. Maybe that's why he hasn't cracked a smile. Maybe he's miserable, furious, and stuck. I can't help but see the similarities between him and Polly.

Now that my fairy-tale fantasy of the royal life is permanently tarnished, I see there's nothing different about these people other than the circumstances of their birth. And I of all people, being an orphan, can't judge someone based on something like that, so completely out of your control.

I gaze at the fountain for a moment, searching for answers. *Go or stay?*

I'll flip a coin. I dig a quarter from my small purse and walk closer to the fountain's light, close my eyes, and toss it in the air.

"Making a wish?" a deep masculine voice asks.

I jump and let out an embarrassing squeak. Speak of the devil. "What're you doing here?"

Gabriel lifts a brow and crosses his arms. "I live here." He's still in his dark blue suit, and the blazer pulls tight across his muscular shoulders and biceps. It's embarrassing how much I want to see him shirtless. Virgin princesses don't go there. Yup, Polly is a virgin. It's mandatory for a princess to be a virgin upon marriage in her old-school kingdom. She abided by the rule not only because she was always accompanied by a chaperone and had romantic visions of her future groom, it's something the royal doctor checks prior to the ceremony. *Blech.*

I meet his eyes. "Do you always take walks at night?"

"Do you?"

"I have a lot on my mind. A hard decision to make."

"Tell me. Maybe I can help."

I stare at him, surprised at his offer. "Thanks, but I have to figure it out myself."

He inclines his head. "If you could make a wish, what would it be?"

I instantly think of Mike, my foster dad, and blurt, "I'd find a cure for cancer."

His eyes are sympathetic, and he steps closer, dropping his arms by his sides. "Is it someone close to you?"

I nod. "My dad." Mike is the closest thing I ever had to a dad. He was diagnosed with advanced lung cancer a year before his retirement. So unfair. "He's too young to die."

He nods gravely. "It is unfair. Unfortunately, I'm dealing with similar…" He clenches his jaw and looks off in the distance toward the sea.

"You can tell me. I won't tell a soul."

He glances at me. "I can't share with outsiders."

He takes a seat on the bench, his elbows resting on his knees, his head bowed. In that moment, he's not a prince, he's a man carrying a heavy burden and a pain I know in my own heart, the grief of impending loss. The helplessness of it all, watching someone you love suffer.

I join him on the bench. "Cancer sucks."

"It does." He straightens and stares straight ahead, his voice hoarse. "He's only fifty-four."

Pain seems to radiate from him, and I scoot closer, leaning against his side in a gesture of comfort. He doesn't pull away. We just sit there, pressed arm to arm, thigh to thigh, warmth building between us in the cool night air.

"Is it your dad too?" I'm guessing based on the age.

He nods once.

I don't press for the details. Royal rules probably restrict him from saying as much as he has, which is really unfair because who's he supposed to unload on? He has to be stoic, above it all, but it's a deep kind of pain when you're faced with losing someone you love. Now I know why the king hasn't made an appearance during this competition, while the queen has been very present. The odd nature of this competition must be because it's urgent for Gabriel to marry, to carry on the line. He will be king soon.

I'm sitting by a fountain in the moonlight, pressed against a future king, and all I want to do is hug him. He feels warm and approachable and so much man. Not perfect, not rigid, not even royal. He's vulnerable and hurting.

So I do. I turn, wrap my arms around him in a sideways hug, and squeeze. He doesn't hug me back, but he can't, really, because I've got his arms pinned to his sides.

I let him go and look up at him.

His lips curve into a small smile. "What was that for?"

I lift one shoulder. "Guess I thought you might need a hug."

He arches a brow.

"Maybe I did too," I admit.

He studies me for a moment. "I can't remember the last time I was hugged. It's just not done in my family. Royals are untouchable for the most part."

"Where I come from, we're more touchy-feely."

"Tell me about your kingdom."

I tense. Not just because my knowledge of Polly's kingdom is limited, but also because I don't want to lie to him. We're kind of bonding here. "My home is a wonderful tropical paradise." At least that's how Tampa is for me, a place where my dream of owning my own salon will one day come true. "Is it weird to be called the prize in this competition?"

"You don't think I'm a prize?" His tone is ironic.

"Are you asking if I think you're hot? Absolutely. Are you asking if I think it's normal to offer a prince as a prize in a *Survivor*-lite competition among princesses? No."

He chuckles, a low rumbly sound that warms my heart. I made him laugh! "This was not my idea."

"Then why're you going along with it?"

He lets out a breath and stands. "Duty calls and I must answer. Make that wish, Polly. I hope it comes true."

He leaves just as quietly as he arrived.

I go back to the fountain, turn my back to it, and make a wish, tossing the coin over my shoulder. It hits with a satisfying splash. My wish is simple yet impossible—winning the competition for a real prize that can save Polly.

I make the long trek down to the beach and walk along the sand in the moonlight, thinking how romantic this might be to walk with a lover. Strange thoughts for me. I'm not much for relationships—too much work, too many heavy expectations. And honestly I don't have the time.

My focus has always been on work, earning money toward my own salon and taking care of Mike for as long as I have him. Gabriel and I share that burden of losing someone to disease.

I sit on the beach and watch the waves for so long I almost feel like I'm in a trance.

I jerk into awareness as it hits me—there's only one way forward. And I need Gabriel to make it work.

Gabriel

After my walk through the gardens, I return to the palace and pace the upper floors, restless and agitated as usual over the future. Finally, I'm tired enough to return to my suite. I dismiss the valet, who's eager to whisk my suit away to be cleaned, and tell him I'll hand over the suit in the morning. Right now I just need to be alone. I shrug off my suit jacket and toss it over the back of a leather high-back chair in the living room.

This competition is wearing on me already. I did my best to entertain our guests after dinner. We retired to the parlor, where I nursed a brandy, making an effort to keep up my end of the conversation, which wasn't easy. The remaining seven women practically rendered me catatonic with their inane chatter. I didn't miss Polly slipping away after dinner either. She didn't care enough about becoming my wife to spend time with me given the opportunity, which was incredibly rude.

Yet, much later, when I excused myself from the chattering princesses and went for a walk, I found myself drawn to her. There she was, standing in the moonlight by the fountain, a vision of wild curls and sweet curves. She seemed like she belonged there, like she should be part of the fantastical fountain with its cheerful glowing lights and playful fish.

I loosen my tie, irritated with myself for fixating on her. She's not a good match for me, the queen has already declared her inappropriate, and I can't say I disagree. Maybe it's because she's so different from anyone I've ever met, and that makes her inherently more interesting. Maybe it's because she's beautiful. Maybe it's because—

She hugged me.

And I liked it. She actually seemed to care about what was going on with me on a deep level. She's losing someone too, understands what that's like—the agony of standing helplessly nearby, unable to do anything. She comforted me, and I welcomed it. I don't even share that burden with my younger siblings. Most of them—five of the six—have apartments at the palace, but they're all full-grown with access to the private jet, so they come and go frequently. They know our father is ill, but they don't know he's gotten worse. The protective big brother in me has kept them in the dark, letting them enjoy their carefree lives, as my father wanted for them. That's probably why my parents haven't called them home yet. My father sees himself in them, being the younger siblings, and has always given them loads of freedom with very few responsibilities.

My mind wanders back to Polly's arrival at the palace. She said I'm a stick-in-the-mud that never leaves the palace. Both of which are untrue. I travel when I get the urge, usually in disguise. I can't relax with the press following me, documenting every move. I have a few women I can call for a private hookup. They've signed nondisclosures and keep the details to themselves. I've been under the harsh glare of public scrutiny my whole life, and after a small indiscretion involving too much drink and my fists (and a not so small one), I've stayed out of the spotlight as much as possible.

My time will come soon enough as king. Even the royal duties I perform as the crown prince are kept private, only for the islanders, no press allowed. Cameras and phones are banned. The queen despises the tawdriness of internet sensations and social media. And she doesn't have to look any further than my younger brother Phillip. He has a huge online following as the royal hottie and has no qualms about being in the spotlight. First with his serious girlfriend as the golden couple and later rutting his way through Europe with the elite. My father always says Phillip is like him before he settled down. Chip off the royal diamond. Ha!

I undo the buttons on my dress shirt cuffs before working down the front, suddenly drained. I'm still young; thirty is my prime, so I shouldn't feel so worn down. The weight of the kingdom is on my shoulders, yes, but I've always known this was my legacy. I am as prepared as a person could be. It would be good to find a partner, someone who could carry the burden with me. Someone who would offer comfort during difficult times.

Like Polly.

I toss my shirt with the jacket, kick off my shoes, and head through my bedroom and into the en suite bathroom for a long steamy shower. A few minutes later, I'm feeling a lot more relaxed, tilting my head back into the spray. An image of Polly flashes through my mind. Her bikini cupping her round perky breasts, smooth tanned skin, toned stomach, curvy hips, long legs, that ass. That perfect round ass meant for a man's hands. I shake my head, ordering myself not to fixate on her. It's a losing battle, and now I'm tense again and hard at the same time. I'm debating taking myself in hand when I hear a noise in my bedroom. Has the valet returned to take my suit? I left the trousers on the bathroom counter.

I grind my teeth. I should've locked the door. I turn off the shower, grab a towel, wrap it around my waist, snag the trousers, and march to the bathroom door, trying to tamp down my temper. He's just doing his job. I poke my head out. "Andrew, here's the…" I trail off, momentarily speechless.

Polly with the wild curls, with the perfect ass, is sitting on my bed, her legs crossed, looking completely at ease. She's wearing a red satin robe that ends high on her thighs, with cheetah heels. My mouth goes dry. Is she naked under that robe? Is she here for what I hope she's here for?

"Hello, handsome," she says cheerfully, swinging one shapely leg. "I was hoping to see those shoulders. Just as magnificent as I imagined. And the water is just glistening —" she wiggles her fingers at me "—running in rivulets down spectacular pecs, six-pack abs, and a glorious happy trail." Her eyes eat me up. Unbelievably brash. She stares at my rapidly rising cock through the towel. "Yup." Her voice is hoarse.

I should be pissed that she dared breach the privacy of my rooms, but instead I'm incredibly turned on. Blame it on the shower. Blame it on the bikini. I blame her.

I toss the trousers on the dresser and approach her. "How did you get in here?"

She lifts one shoulder. "Door was unlocked."

"How did you know which room was mine?"

She smiles, her teeth flashing white against luscious red lips. "It took a few guesses. I pretended I got lost and was looking for my room. I knew you wouldn't be in the wing with all of us. And one of the servants told me the bedrooms were on the second and third floors. The floors above that are for servants, the nursery, and storage." She frowns. "You grew up in an attic? That's almost worse than the crappy places I landed. I mean, considering there was so much luxury all around you."

A princess landed in a crappy place? My testosterone-flooded brain goes right back to the most important thing —Polly is practically naked, sitting on my bed, ripe for the picking. I should care why she's here because she could be planning some kind of treachery, but with those big sparkling brown eyes, her easy smile, her soft-looking skin, her luscious curves, none of that seems to matter.

"Should I dress?" *Or remove this towel?*

She stares at my bicep. "Only if you want. I'm enjoying the view."

I sit next to her on the mattress, my thigh close enough to brush the satin of her robe.

She looks up at me, her voice husky. "You might be wondering why I'm here."

"Not really."

Her eyes widen. "A woman appears in the middle of the night in your private royal room and you don't wonder why she's there? What if I had a knife? What if I planned an assassination?"

My lips twitch. "Do you have a knife?"

"No." She purses her lips, sexy as all hell. "But you shouldn't be so trusting."

"You did hug me before."

"True."

I stare at her mouth, and her luscious lips part, her pink tongue darting out to lick them. A surge of lust rushes through me. She wants me to kiss her. "I thought it was pretty obvious why you're here."

She lifts a hand near my face and then drops it, muttering to herself about Polly. She's a strange one, referring to herself in the third person. Ask me if I care.

I brush her curls over her shoulder. They feel springy like I could pull them and they'd bounce.

She stands abruptly and faces me. "I have a few things to say."

She's a talker. Great. Just what I need after hours of princess chatter.

"Go on." I head to my dresser for some boxer briefs. If we're going to talk, at least I can get out of this wet towel. I pull the briefs up under the towel, take off the towel, dry off as best I can, and set it on the dresser. She still hasn't said a word. I turn. "Why aren't you talking?"

Her gaze darts all over my body like she can't decide where to look, but she can't look away. This pleases me. "I am loving this view even more," she says with great enthusiasm, her voice breathy. "Do you always wear just briefs in front of a strange woman who wanders into your private room for possibly nefarious purposes?"

I find myself smiling, a rare laugh bubbling up. "I don't usually have a strange woman wander into my private room for possibly nefarious purposes, so I can't say that I always do."

She swallows, the movement in her long neck mesmerizing; then she lifts her chin and meets my eyes. "Oh, wow, now *those* are bedroom eyes." Her gaze drops to my tenting briefs. "And bedroom briefs."

I bark out a laugh. She slays me.

She laughs too. "I've been wanting to make you laugh since I arrived. Maybe you're not such a stick-in-the-mud."

I stop smiling. "Maybe?"

She grimaces. "I'm sorry I said that before. I was a little flustered because you were in a tux and very tense like every butler I ever saw—" she coughs "—and, at the same time, you were so young and hot." She waves a hand up and down my body, and there is no way this erection is going anywhere when she keeps complimenting me and looking at it. "You must've been in a bad mood at the time because this whole crazy competition was about to unleash on you."

"Not to mention the furry wedding."

She laughs and pats the bed next to her. "Now that's a story I need to hear."

I sit next to her and tell her the whole sorry tale. It's not like it's a secret. The wedding travesty will be in *Luxury Weddings* and *Bride Special* magazines soon. *Thanks again for that, Phillip.* He disappeared right along with the wedding people, abandoning me to deal with our parents alone during this insane time, along with a pack of bridal hopefuls. He could've at least run interference with our parents. Jerk. He's probably rutting away in some posh hotel in Paris. I fill Polly in on Phillip's insistence on opening up the palace and my insistence on preserving our history and tradition.

Polly's eyes are wide when I finish. "Back it up. Did you say a giant purple bunny kept hopping by among all the native Australian species? Kangaroo, koala, wombat, dingoes, and a giant purple bunny?"

"Yes," I bite out. She was supposed to take my side on preserving our history. Instead she's fixated on the furry abomination.

She bursts out laughing. "Classic! I love it!" She's laughing so hard tears are coming out of her eyes.

My lips curve despite the horrid furry situation because she's just so…fun and open and affectionate. Everything I'm not. I suddenly feel like I'm missing that in my life, like I need it. I need her.

She wipes her eyes and blows out a breath. "Woo! That was some story. Now I see where you were at when we first met. Tough times." She giggles. "Sorry. I'm sure it was truly an abomination—" another giggle "—as you said."

"It wasn't that funny."

She bobs her head, holds up a finger, and takes a deep breath in and out. "Okay, I'm calm now. So, the reason I'm here. I think we can help each other out."

I drop my voice to a husky tone. "I think so too."

She stands and moves over near the dresser. I instantly feel the loss, the distance between us.

She holds up a palm as if trying to ward off my advance though I haven't moved. "I'm here to help you. Those other princesses are like piranhas, all trying to get a bite out of you. I'm much more low key."

"You're low key?" I ask incredulously, thinking of her typically loud clothes and brash manners. The woman snuck into my bedroom, for crying out loud.

She glares at me. "Yes. What's that supposed to mean?"

"Nothing. Do go on." I can't remember the last time I was so turned on and entertained at the same time.

She paces in front of the dresser, stops, and stares at my wet towel on top of it. "This is an antique," she says before grabbing the towel and heading into the bathroom. She returns sans towel and declares, "You help me win the competition, and that will end it quickly with very little fuss. I won't eat you alive. I'll just be my low-key self and let you do your royal thing."

My mind latches on to the last part. *Your royal thing*. What a strange way to put it. Isn't it her royal thing too? It's like she wasn't raised properly in the royal tradition. No wonder she sounds so unrefined. Her people have failed her. Still, it only makes clear that I can't help her win the competition. She would never be accepted as queen, my mother wouldn't allow it, and my father would follow suit. They've always been a united front. And it wouldn't be fair to Polly. She's completely unprepared for the job. Truth? If I could live as a free man, she's exactly the kind of beautiful free spirit I'd want. And the sad irony is I didn't know I wanted that until I met *her*.

But I'm not a free man. I'm heir to a kingdom, and if I'm selfish and choose her and help her win this competition, she would be miserable. I'd be a complete jerk to allow it. Not only would all the duties and rules expected of the queen destroy her spirit, it would be an enormous heavy responsibility and a lot of hard work. My queen will have to help me save a kingdom. A princess can enjoy certain freedoms. She cannot be queen.

"I don't want to marry you," I say gently.

Her brown eyes flash, giving me a jolt. "Why not?"

I give her only part of it, trying to spare her feelings.

She doesn't need to know that the queen has already declared her a bad fit. "You haven't been raised properly."

She slams her hands on her hips and tosses her hair. She's magnificent. "Rude!"

I slowly stand to my full height and stalk toward her.

She lifts her chin. "Fine. I'll feed you to the wolves if that's what you want."

I close the distance, backing her up to the wall, caging her in, my palms flat on the wall behind her. I dip my head to speak directly in her ear. "*I* am the wolf and I want you."

She shivers. "That's bold."

I shift, her lips mere millimeters away when she turns her head and ducks under my arm.

"And no," she says, standing much too far away.

"Why not?" I bark. I usually have better control, but need claws at me.

She huffs. "Because you don't get everything you want when you want it, *Your Highness*." She says that last part with pure contempt. I've never been addressed so rudely. I still want her.

She goes on, her hands gesturing wildly. "Before you were so rude, I was going to suggest you help me win the game, and in return, you give me some compensation to quietly disappear."

I blink. "You want me to pay you to leave?" *You don't want to marry me?*

"Yes."

"Why?"

Her eyes shift to the side before meeting my eyes. "Reasons."

"I need a bride regardless. There will be no compensation. The best candidate will win."

She looks to the ceiling, her hands in fists, apparently trying to get her temper under control. She levels a fiery look my way. "And you don't care who that is?" *Is she jealous?*

"Of course I care, but it's not a simple thing. There's a way it must be done. You must understand adhering to royal traditions."

Her lips form a flat line. "I don't understand anything about the way you do things here. Pitting princesses against each other? You don't like this any more than I do, so let's work together to end it."

"There are circumstances you don't understand, and I'm sorry, but I can't explain any further than that."

She throws her hands up. "Fine! But don't expect me to help you out with your lusty urges. I'm a virgin." She looks away, like she's lying. No one with her brash open sensuality could possibly be inexperienced. Would a virgin seek out my bedroom? Plus she's got to be in her twenties, which is a long time to still be a virgin.

I close the distance. "How old are you?"

"Twenty-three." She slowly backs up, veering closer to the foot of the four-poster bed. "It's the rule in my kingdom. Princesses must be virgins upon marriage."

If she is a virgin, then I absolutely should not touch her. I should show her the door, eliminate temptation.

"Polly." I capture her wrists and hold them behind the wooden post at the foot of my bed, leaning into her space. I can't seem to help myself. I breathe in her spicy floral scent, dying for a taste of her.

Her chest rises and falls rapidly, cleavage peeking out of the top of her robe. Her face tips up, meeting my eyes with raw desire.

I slowly lean down, and she keeps her eyes open, her

pupils are black and large, gold specks in the dark irises. Beautiful. Her lashes lower as I brush my lips over hers lightly, once, twice. I release her wrists and lift my head, giving her ample time to step away.

She makes a frustrated sound, grabs my head, and kisses me again. *Yes!* Her lips are yielding, soft, and she tastes like mint and something uniquely her, a spicy edge. My world narrows down to this kiss, almost innocent in its delicious decadence. A slow carnal invitation to more. I thrust my tongue into her mouth, and hers slides along mine. Slow, deep, wet kisses. I'm drowning in sensation, drunk on her lusciousness.

She lifts her hips, pressing herself against me, and the kiss turns raw, carnal, hungry. I slip my leg between hers, giving her pressure, and her head tilts back on a moan.

Every nerve ending crackles to life as I dive in for more of her luscious mouth, the blood roaring in my ears. Closer, I need to get closer. I press my aching hardness against her softness, the urge to claim her powerful, a primal instinct that clouds my thinking. I'm nothing but throbbing raw need. I want her more than I've ever wanted anyone in my life, and I want her now. A small niggling worry over her virgin status gives me pause.

I break the kiss, and she remains leaning against the post, her lips rosy, her cheeks flushed. So fucking sexy.

"I want you." My voice is rough with lust. "Stay the night or leave now."

Our gazes lock, hot, intense. She's taking my measure, and I'm teetering on the sharp edge of need. Seconds tick by, the tension palpable in the air.

She shoves me back with both hands on my chest. "And that's my cue." She walks briskly toward the door.

Then she stops, turns, and says softly, "Goodnight, Gabriel."

She said my name. Not Your Highness. And she said it with a hint of longing.

"Goodnight, Polly. The offer stands for another night if you change your mind. I'll leave the door unlocked."

The door quietly shuts behind her.

Fuck. Maybe she really is a virgin. I have to keep my hands to myself. Back to the shower for me.

6

____

Anna

I'm sipping coffee in the parlor after a huge breakfast, hoping a shiny idea will crack through the muddle of my brain. The other princesses are picking at fruit or eating nothing at all, most of them opting for tea. They're so dainty and refined. It must've been awful to have the spark squashed out of you as a kid. I'd almost feel sorry for them if they weren't so bitchy toward me. Is it my accent? It's like they think I'm the lowest princess on the totem pole. Maybe Polly is. I'm not up on the royal hierarchy.

I had a restless night, reliving the wonder of Gabriel. I have never seen such a beautiful man in real life—glistening golden muscles that made me want to run my tongue all over him, lapping up every last drop of water from his shower or join him in there. He's so comfortable in his own skin that he just stood practically naked in front of me with complete casualness. And that kiss, my Lord, I have never been kissed like that before. Like he wanted to devour me, and it was so mutual. This is the kind of passion I thought only existed in the movies. I flush hot just thinking about it.

So what to do with what I have? The crown prince is hot for me. He doesn't want to help me win. Or marry me. I don't know why, but that burns. I mean, it's one thing for me to decide we're from two different worlds, I know who I really am, but he thinks I'm a princess. How dare he say I wasn't raised properly! Just because I show my bare shoulders (gasp!) or because I show up in a prince's bedroom in the middle of the night? Well, maybe that did give the wrong impression. But I corrected course and told him I was a virgin.

Hmm…the only thing I can think of to achieve Operation Save Polly is to win the treasure hunt today. Maybe it's for something valuable like a diamond, something I can pawn for enough bucks for a fancy lawyer. I just can't let a defenseless dove like Polly be trapped in a cage.

The actual butler, Nolan, steps forward (not quite my hoped-for Jeeves, Nigel, or Edwin—another royal fantasy crushed). He's probably forties with a full head of dark hair neatly parted to the side. Serious and dignified, but not stuffy. At least he wears a black suit. "Please report to the entrance hall. The queen will greet you there."

I take a last sip of coffee while the princesses take their leave, trailing in a graceful line to the door. All perfect poise and manners. Ha! I saw them in action yesterday. It won't take long before they turn savage, especially now that Gabriel is the ultimate prize. My gut clenches, and I force my mind back to my purpose here—win the treasure, save Polly.

I catch up with the group in the marble entrance hall. We're waiting on the queen. I turn to Elizabeth, the red-haired princess. "What do you think the treasure is?"

Her pink lips tighten and she stares straight ahead. "It's not polite to speak of money."

"You think it's money?"

"No."

"Jewels?"

She shakes her head and lowers her voice. "Nothing is as it seems. Look deeper."

I nod sagely. "Right." Clearly she's trying to help me. What does she see that I'm missing? I'm intrigued by the royal intrigue. Also irritated. I need answers. I need to know if this is worth my time. Maybe I should go back home and beg Polly to call her family for help, even though she doesn't want them to know. But what if they disown her like she fears? The burden of her potential imprisonment weighs heavily on me. She's my only family, and I'm all she's got right now. *Hang in there, Polly!*

The queen arrives, trailed by the same servants who helped her with yesterday's competition. It occurs to me a daily competition could whittle down the princess candidates by the end of the week. What happens to the last princess standing in those remaining two weeks? A royal gauntlet of tests? Royal conjugal visits testing compatibility? So many questions I'm not sure I want to know the answers to.

The women instantly quiet and bow their heads, curtsying to the queen. I do the same a split second later. Look at me practically blending, and it's only my second day.

"Good morning," the queen says brightly. "You'll be traveling to the port today, where bicycles are waiting for you on the dock."

A few of the princesses exchange worried looks.

Marguerite speaks up. "Your Majesty, I thought we spoke of horses last night."

The queen narrows her eyes. "I am the final judge in this competition, which means I make the rules."

Marguerite lowers her eyes to the ground. "I don't know how to ride a bicycle, ma'am."

"Then you shall walk." The queen takes in the rest of us. "Anyone else not know how to ride a bicycle?"

Slowly hands go up. Four of them. Poor deprived princesses.

The queen indicates the elderly servant standing close by. "Albert will teach you how to ride, and then off you go."

Damn, that's harsh. *Suckers.*

The bicycle-deficient princesses are quiet and gloomy, but the other three are chattering happily. The queen looks displeased at the noise.

I take the opportunity to ask my question while she's already irritated at the others. "Your Majesty, what's the treasure?"

The queen purses her lips like she sucked a sour lemon. Guess that was one question too many. "That is for the winner to know."

"Can you ballpark the cash value?" I blurt.

"One more rude remark from you and you're out," the queen snaps.

The women stare at me in shock. Apparently, speaking of money really is forbidden, even when you're on a treasure hunt. Obviously treasure has some cash value, right?

The queen dismisses us in her haughty royal way, but I don't miss the small smile on her lips. She's enjoying the hell out of the game.

The eight of us princesses head out the palace doors and over to the road, where three black Mercedes with tinted windows are waiting. I slip into the backseat of one with Francesca and Marguerite. They're on either side of me—a princess sandwich.

Francesca is a dark-haired princess from a kingdom somewhere in the Middle East I've never heard of. She's quiet, but her dark eyes are sharp and calculating. Here I thought Marguerite was the one to watch, but up close I can see there might be more princesses to consider as serious competition. Elizabeth was right, I do need to look deeper.

A horrible thought strikes in this whole look-deeper thing. Crap. Do not even tell me this treasure is symbolic. I will seriously raise hell if I go through this whole hunt for something deep like "the treasure was within you all along" or "the treasure is nature itself."

I turn to Marguerite. "I thought since you came up with today's competition, you might be granted immunity and just watch."

She shakes her head. "The queen does as she wishes. I'll bet the clues aren't even drawn from nature like I suggested. She already traded horses for bicycles. Who knows if there's even a treasure?"

"You think it's fake?"

Francesca adds her two quiet cents. "All that matters is who wins."

"Oh, shut up," Marguerite snaps.

Francesca turns a lethal glare onto Marguerite, and I suddenly wish I weren't between them. I've seen these women in action. They go for blood and fight dirty, no clean punches.

A stony silence falls, the women each looking out their window.

I breathe a sigh of relief. A few moments later, my mind drifts back to Gabriel, as you do when you've seen him practically naked with those magnificent shoulders, glorious chest, his massive…bulge. I want him, even though I shouldn't. He's not a stick-in-the-mud rigid royal. He's a man in difficult circumstances, doing his duty regardless. A man of honor. Damn. I shouldn't have said I'm a virgin because a man of honor would never cross that line. Maybe I can convince him to do other stuff. Oh, man, I am the worst. Here I am, thinking of my own lusty needs. So what if I haven't had sex in a year? That doesn't mean I break character and have my way with the crown prince. Unless…

What if I did? Would it get me kicked out of the competition? Would he show me the door himself?

Stop that! You're here for Polly, not yourself.

But I might never have a chance to be with his spectacularly hot body again. And, of course, we'd talk. I'm not just about the body. Dirty, raunchy talk.

I'm startled out of my sexy X-rated fantasy when the car comes to a halt. I hadn't even gotten to the good part yet. Anyway, we just parked by the dock, and it's another perfect sunny June day on the island with a sparkling blue-green sea and bright blue skies with white fluffy clouds. Paradise. *It's no Tampa, but…*

I join the princesses over where a group of bicycles wait. The bikes are cute, red with upright handles, a cushy wide seat, and a basket on the front. I claim one and then have to wait while Albert attempts to teach four princesses how to ride a bike. Albert is too old and stooped to run behind them holding the seat as they pedal, the way most kids learn. Instead he instructs them and waits, looking hopeful.

Pedal, crash! One princess down.

Crash! Another down. She didn't even get to the pedaling.

The other two princesses balk.

"You must try, Your Royal Highnesses," Albert urges. "The clues are all over the island. It's too much ground to cover on foot." When nobody moves, he adds, "The queen will be displeased if you don't follow the rules."

That gets the princesses moving. I'll say this for them, they really do try. Skinned knees and all, even a few colorful swear words. But after an hour, even I can tell it's just not going to happen. And poor Albert is red in the face from barking out orders, his scraggly white hair disheveled from running his hands through it in frustration.

I stand from where I've been sitting on the ground, cross-legged, and stretch. "What if those of us who know how to ride give the others a lift? You could sit on the handlebars or on the seat if we stand to pedal."

Marguerite, one of the bicycle-deprived princesses, points at me. "Yes! Let's do that."

The three princesses who actually know how to ride promptly refuse. It's every princess for herself out here.

In the end, the four of us take off on our bikes, and the other four, well, they run. And that's quite a sight for the islanders, who come out of their cute cottages to see princesses break all manner of decorum to run in the most awkward display of athleticism I've ever witnessed. They look like a bunch of five-year-olds, running full out with flailing arms. If only I still had my phone to video it. This shit is gold.

∾

Gabriel

If my father weren't so ill and my mother so distraught, I would never play along with this ridiculous game. But my parents are truly happy, smiling for the first time in a good year, which is the only reason I'm standing in the shadows of a cave on the far side of the island, waiting for the princess—the winner—who's figured out the final clue. My only consolation is that the games will be over soon. My mother cannot help herself from continuing the daily competitions. She and my father are enjoying themselves too much. Yesterday she sent two princesses packing. If she keeps that up, two leaving every day, it'll be narrowed down to two by the weekend. What she plans to do with the last two for the next two weeks makes me uneasy. She could pit them against each other. She could test each of them separately. Or the more likely answer, which I'm really trying not to think about, is that she has them go on dates with me à la *The Bachelor*. Knowing the final choice is not entirely up to me, I don't see why I have to go through all the work of entertaining them. Polly would entertain me just by being herself. *Stop fixating on her.* I know she cannot be queen, but ever since our kiss, hell, even before that, the first time I laid eyes on her, I was drawn to her. I dreamed of her cheetah heel clocking me on the jaw in the heat of passion the very first night she arrived.

I looked her up online last night. She's from Beaumont, a chain of tropical islands in the Caribbean with a thriving tourist industry. The few pictures of her show her in hats with veils over her face for modesty, smiling, her dark curly hair tied back. The monarchy on Beaumont has done well in keeping strict adherence to tradition and is well revered by its people. My mind keeps turning over the puzzle of Polly. If she comes from a good traditional family, why does she seem so far from the royal mold? The only thing I can think of is that her time in the US for her education gave her a taste of a different life, and upon return to her traditional home, she went through a rebellious stage. How else to explain her revealing clothes and complete lack of restraint? She says what she wants, does what she wants. She seems very open and free.

Could she manage the role of queen? Or would it represent everything she's trying to get away from?

I take a seat on a flat rock. This has got to be the strangest treasure hunt in the history of treasure hunts—a series of athletic challenges leads to each clue before finally leading to the treasure. My mother completely disregarded the tame suggestion from Marguerite to use nature as clues. My father came up with the challenges and was quite giddy about it, from what I heard. He was always an athlete at heart. Unfortunately, that is not what these princesses have been raised to be. Sure, they may excel on horseback, but cycling? Throwing a shot put? Kicking a ball past the goalie? I don't even know what else. I stopped watching on the closed-circuit TV when Marguerite kneed the goalie (poor William) in the nuts, picked up the ball, and tossed it in the net, apparently forgetting she was supposed to kick the ball in. She should be out for unsportsmanlike conduct, but the king and queen find her too entertaining to dismiss. My father laughed until he cried.

Polly was amazing to watch earlier. Once she realized the athletics involved, she put her high-heeled sandals in the bicycle basket and did the remainder barefoot. She kicked that ball hard too, using the side of her foot. It sailed right past William.

I was told three of them were working on the last clue, which would lead to a hike to this cave, balancing a stack of blocks on their head. The things my father thought up! At least his mind still works, even while his body is failing him.

I'm in the shadows, so they won't see me until I want to be seen. The camera is at the entrance to the cave and doesn't reach this far back, which lets me relax. I played in this cave as a boy with my younger siblings. There are ledges and hideaways, perfect for a clubhouse or, when we were older, privacy for meeting a girl. That was before the hammer came down over nondisclosures and keeping the royal gift covered. Ah, the stupid carefree days of youth.

Suddenly my younger brother by a year, Phillip, appears, grinning ear to ear. "Well, well," he chortles, stepping into the cave, smiling some more at me.

Before he can get a jab in about my active participation in this ludicrous game, I close the distance and growl, "Where have you been?"

He brought an insane wedding planner into our home and let her run wild with a wedding full of people in stuffed-animal suits. And then the wedding planner, who claimed to be some by-blow of a previous king, sabotaged a second wedding on the same day. The palace was in chaos, and then Phillip disappeared right along with the wedding planner.

"Nice to see you too," he says. "I wanted to lie low after that furry wedding debacle, and I knew you were pissed about the wedding planner I hired. I went to Monte Carlo to see Adrian."

Adrian, our youngest brother, is a card shark. He loves a good high-stakes poker game.

I spear a hand through my hair. "Did you know about this bridal competition?"

He hesitates, and I have my answer.

"Fuck, why didn't you warn me?"

"I couldn't tell you. You were already so mad about the wedding stuff. I thought you'd have a conniption over the bridal competition, and I didn't want that anger directed at me. It wasn't *my* idea."

I shake my head. We haven't brawled in years. I'm above that now. Mostly.

He turns to look out the cave entrance—still no princesses—and turns back to me. "So…here we are. What made you go along with it?"

I straighten my spine. "It's my duty."

"Your duty is to hide in a cave?"

"Fuck you." I don't put a lot of heat into it because I'm actually glad he's back. Being so close in age, we've always been tight. And he's one of the few people not put off by my sometimes gruff manner. I blame it on my Viking ancestors. I should be leading men into battle or conquering new worlds. Instead I'm bound by civilized royal tradition. It takes great strength to do one's duty, to think of the greater good of your country, of your family, above yourself. That doesn't mean it's easy.

He smiles. "One more thing. Our brothers and sisters have been summoned. They're supposed to check out the remaining two candidates this weekend."

I go cold. I'm sure they've been summoned because of our father's declining health too. It will be difficult and painful for everyone involved. I keep that to myself.

"Wonderful," I snarl. "Everyone should have a say in my wife."

He claps a hand on my shoulder. "Stay strong, brother."

I can hear the smile in his voice, even if he's wise enough not to let it show on his face. I barely resist slapping him upside the head. "Piss off."

He leaves, chuckling to himself. I return to my flat rock in the shadows to contemplate the indignity of my life.

A short while later, Marguerite comes into view, walking carefully along the shifting sands of the dune. No one else is in sight. A block falls off the stack of three on her head, but she doesn't bow out like she's supposed to for failing the task, she keeps going. I see now this was the true test. Full effort by the rules or bow out. The queen of Villroy does nothing halfway and must follow the rules prescribed by royal traditions. Marguerite definitely can't win now, entertaining or not.

A blond woman comes into view behind Marguerite, and I'm shockingly disappointed not to see wild dark curls. I thought Polly would have this locked down since she's the most athletic. The blond woman suddenly falls to the ground, her ankle twisting in the shifting sand, the blocks scattered around her. A moment later, she carefully stands and limps away, bowing out.

Marguerite is nearly upon me when Polly makes her way up the dune. I'm on my feet, silently cheering for my horse in the race.

They're neck and neck within seconds because Polly is strong and determined. They both stop short at the cave entrance. Marguerite tilts her head, letting the remaining blocks fall. The challenge was to scale the sandy dune with the blocks balanced on their head, so the blocks are no longer required.

Polly neatly plucks the blocks off her own head and sets them on the ground. "This is the final clue, the cave."

Marguerite's brows furrow. "The treasure's in a cave? You go in."

"Then you forfeit?"

"Just check if there are any bats or snakes in there. Then we'll both go in."

Polly shakes her head. "If I go in first, I'm getting the treasure." She's matter-of-fact, not angry about Marguerite throwing her to the hazards of an unknown cave. Like me. Ha.

They both stare at the cave. I wait, silently urging Polly to take the lead. *Nothing in here but us hungry wolves.*

Polly turns to Marguerite. "You think there's spiders in there? I mean, I don't care about bats. They're sleeping in the daytime like cute little mouse vampires. But spiders?" She shivers.

"This is silly," Marguerite says. "I'll go." She takes a step forward and turns back to Polly. "Are the snakes around here poisonous?"

"Relax, I'll go. If anyone's going to be devoured by a giant anaconda, it should be me. After all, I'm the lowest princess on the totem pole."

I clench my jaw. She shouldn't talk about herself like that.

Marguerite is still working her angle. "Bring the treasure out, and you can keep most of it."

News flash, ladies, you can't have only most of me.

Polly tilts her head, considering. "If I do that, I'll be the winner. You'll be second place."

"That works. I'm not worried. There's still weeks left of the competition, and I was first place yesterday." The whole negotiation is surprisingly cordial and restrained.

Another woman appears on the dune.

"Go!" Marguerite hollers, giving Polly a shove.

Polly takes off like a shot into the cave.

I step forward into the light, and she throws her hands in the air and screams bloody murder.

"Relax, it's just me," I say.

She smacks my shoulder repeatedly. "You scared the shit out of me! What're you doing skulking around caves for? Where's the treasure?"

Somehow I know this isn't going to go over well. She really wants some kind of compensation for her efforts. I don't know why exactly, but I give her the benefit of the doubt that it's for a good reason. I fear I'm halfway in love with her. One hug, one kiss, and I'm a goner. All because of her and her rebellious free spirit.

I take her hand. "Follow me."

She follows me into the darkness, and I pull her close, my arms lightly wrapped around her. She's trembling. I really did scare her. "I'm sorry I startled you."

Her arms wrap tightly around my waist, and she presses her cheek to my chest. Then, seeming to realize she's hugging me, she suddenly drops her arms and lifts her head. "It's fine. Just point me in the direction of the treasure."

I tighten my hold on her, hugging her or restraining her, I'm not sure. All I know is she'll be furious when she hears the treasure news. I do the only thing I can think of in these circumstances, holding a feisty sexy woman in a dark cave, I kiss her, one hand on her jaw, holding her in place, my arm banding around her waist, keeping her close. It's a hard demanding kiss meant to distract her, and she responds like I lit a fire under her. Our tongues do battle as her fingers tunnel into my hair, and her leg lifts and wraps around mine. It's the hottest kiss of my life, urgent and wild. I'm rock hard. I cup her firm ass, pressing her against my aching groin.

"Did you find it?" Marguerite calls into the cave. "Are you still alive?"

Polly breaks the kiss, breathing hard. "Fuck me," she whispers in a low curse. "You're the treasure, aren't you?"

I drop my hold on her and hold my temper in check, speaking in a fierce low tone. "You don't need to sound so disappointed."

She speaks in an equally fierce low tone. "I need *real* treasure. Gold, jewels, cash."

I stiffen, doubting her for the first time. She sounds mercenary, and I know her kingdom has a thriving economy. "What do you need it for?"

"My kingdom."

"They're doing well with tourism already."

"It's not the country I'm helping. It's a person. A really important person to the kingdom."

And I'm in the same place, going through all of this to help my father, the king, to bring him some joy in his last days and peace of mind for the succession. Polly and I are cut from the same cloth—duty, honor, obligation. Others above ourselves.

Polly sets her hands on my shoulders and goes up on tiptoe to whisper directly in my ear. Her breasts press against my chest and arm. I am not unaffected. "You see why my offer makes sense? You help me win, pay me, and you're free to marry the woman of your choice."

She doesn't want to marry me, and that should make everything easy and clear, except I'm not ready to let her go. My hands go to her waist, spreading my fingers to feel as much of her heat through her shirt as I can. "I have never had the freedom to marry the woman of my choice. Let's go. You'll be declared the winner."

"What did I win?" she asks softly. "I have nothing to show for it."

Irritated by her lack of appreciation and by the whole absurd situation that is my life, I grab her hand and drag her out of the cave and into the light of day. Three princesses stand there, their eyes huge at seeing me. "Polly is the winner. I am the treasure. She'll have dinner with me this evening."

"Congratulations," they murmur in near unison, shooting her jealous looks. These ladies would've been happy to have me as the treasure.

Polly looks off in the distance, and I can almost see the gears turning in her mind. She is single-minded in her determination to send funds to this person back home. I will help her, but not until I'm ready to say goodbye.

7

———

I won the second competition, but it's a hollow victory. I'm no closer to helping the real Polly than I was when I first arrived. The queen has quietly arranged for me to have tea with her in her private sitting room, where, as the winner, I'm expected to name two princesses who should be kicked off the island. I don't care about that. All I care about is having a say in the next challenge so I can arrange for a prize of some value. I'll bow out before we get to the final two contestants. That's what it'll come down to at this rate of competing and eliminating.

My maid, Anna, leads me on a long twisty journey through the palace—I need a map of this place—and I'm escorted into a surprisingly masculine room. Dark wood paneling, floor-to-ceiling bookcases along one wall, burgundy leather sofa with matching wingback chairs. The lighting is warm and dim from a few lamps on side tables. I turn back to Anna, curious if this is the king's sitting room, but I only catch a glimpse of her back as she slips out the door.

I turn back to the cozy room. There's even a fireplace and a small wet bar in the corner. It smells wonderful in here, like paper, leather, and rich woodsy notes. Like a manly wine! I smile at my own joke and walk over to the bookcase. The books are really old; some of them have hand-stitched leather covers. I run my finger down the spine of one.

"That's a boring one," a deep masculine voice says, startling me.

I whirl, my cheeks flushing hot. "I didn't hear you come in."

"I know." Gabriel strides toward me, all masculine swagger. "Too caught up in the history of horse breeding on the island to notice me."

I gulp, the room suddenly airless as he stands directly in front of me. "Where's the queen?"

"Please have a seat." He gestures toward the long leather sofa. "Brandy?"

"No, thanks." I need my wits about me, but then one look at his sexy bedroom eyes and my brain clouds while my heart thumps out a quick answering beat. It goes like this *yes, please, yes, please.* I play it cool despite the X-rated fantasy reel that's been on repeat in my head since last night. "Please tell me you're not trying to seduce me."

"So brash," he mutters, turning on his heel and striding to the sofa. "Don't worry, Anna will be discreet."

He says it like it's a forgone conclusion that he *will* be seducing me. I search for some righteous indignation, but nope. *Nada.* Instead I'm checking him out. He's changed into a light blue button-down shirt that stretches across his broad shoulders, crisp gray pants, and black leather shoes. I'm in a pink halter top and white pencil skirt with my nude sandals. I feel way underdressed. Like I'm wearing a big sign that says commoner. How did we get to this place? Royal versus commoner locked in a battle of lust. It feels like a forgone conclusion to me too, like it had to come to this.

He sought me out. He summoned me to what must be his private sitting room. Why not his bedroom? Did I read this all wrong? Maybe he wants to talk and make an arrangement to help me win.

My brain is too muddled with lust to figure it out, so I go the easy route. I mentally undress him. It's so much more vivid when he's right here. Too bad he's who he is from where he is, and I'm not who he thinks I am. My gut does a slow roll and I look away, fidgeting with the end of my shirt. Guilt stabs at me. I've been lying to him this whole time. He's been good to me, tender even in his gruff way. We've shared some intimate moments, not just physical, a real connection. If he finds out that I'm not Polly, he'll be furious at the betrayal. I shudder to think what might happen to me, or the real Polly for that matter. Banishment, jail time, or worse.

I wish I didn't have to play the part anymore. I wish I could just be me. I'll try as much as I can to be real with him without giving Polly away.

"Polly."

I turn at the name that is me but not me. What would it be like to hear my name from his lips?

He crooks his finger at me from where he stands by the sofa.

I cross to him without a second thought, and he waits for me to sit before taking a seat next to me. I'll say one thing for royalty, they sure do have nice manners. There's some space between us and a definite tension in the air.

I clear my throat. "So what's up?"

He stretches his arms along the back of the sofa, leaning back in a relaxed pose that doesn't fool me for a minute. He's holding himself tightly in check. A man of honor who won't touch a virgin, I remind myself. "I wanted to talk to you about the competition."

I look around the room, searching for cameras. "Is this being filmed?"

"No."

I relax a little and look at him, feeling hopeful. Maybe he really is going to help me win. It'll be hard to leave, knowing I'll never see him again, but at least I'll know I saved Polly.

"Which two princesses do you think we should ask to leave? Many failed at today's challenge."

It's not what I hoped he'd say, but I'm honest. "I'd kick off everyone but Marguerite and Francesca. They have backbones."

He lifts a sardonic brow. "And I need a backbone in a wife?"

I straighten. "Hell yeah. Otherwise they'll be crying into their pillow, worrying you don't love them."

He looks mildly amused, his full lips flirting with a smile that I'm suddenly desperate to see. He lowers his arms from the back of the sofa and leans closer. "And why would they think that?"

"Because your contempt for their weakness would show."

His head jerks back like I've shocked him. Finally he seems to recover himself and informs me coldly, "I would've been content with an arranged marriage through royal channels, as it's always been done."

"That's so sad. Don't you want love and passion?"

His voice is husky, his stunning blue-green eyes warm

on mine. "What do you know of love and passion? Aren't you a virgin?"

My stomach dips. This is a dangerous game. I am not me in these circumstances. I cannot give in to lusty impulses. It's the real Polly who will bear the brunt of my actions. I cross my arms, drawing on brash belligerence. "I know I want it."

"Do you?" he asks silkily.

"Is that all you wanted to talk to me about?" I can't bring myself to ask for compensation again, especially with the heat simmering between us just waiting for the tiniest of sparks to ignite it. I know it would be insanely hot between us, and I also know, deep down, it would be wrong. No matter how much I wish it weren't true. I can't have it both ways—be a virgin princess (in order to save one) and be me taking what I selfishly want.

"Tonight we'll have dinner in my suite," he says. It's not a question. He's a man used to having his demands met promptly and in full. He's the goddamn crown prince of Villroy. One day he will be king.

I ignore his request because he will not be *my* king. He will, some day in the future, be only a fantasy for me, a remembered ache, a longing left unsatisfied. "What about this? The next competition is for all the marbles. Do or die, only one princess left standing. And then she has a choice of you or diamonds."

His jaw clenches so hard I fear he's going to crack a molar. "So it's me or the cash equivalent? And what value would you place on that?"

I bluster on, keenly aware he's close to kicking me out. "You are *way* high on value. Like millions', billions', trillions' worth. Practically priceless."

"And if the winner chooses the millions, then who would be my bride?"

"Runner-up?"

He gives me a cold smile. "I believe the next challenge should involve spiders."

"You'll scare all the women away with that one." I hate that there's a tremor in my voice. Spiders are my one weird phobia. And somehow I don't think Francesca would be scared away. Which would she value more—the crown prince or the cold hard cash?

He stands. "Only the weak."

I leap to my feet at the insult, turn, and stalk toward the door. Pride has me turning back to set him straight. "It's not weak to have a legitimate phobia. Look it up. It's called arachnophobia."

He closes the distance between us alarmingly fast, glowering down at me. "My queen must be fearless, strong, and adhere strictly to the rules. It's clear that is not you."

I lift my chin. "I never wanted to be your queen. I came here for an inheritance. Why can't we keep it simple with real prizes?"

He gives me a smug smile. "There are some who would say *I* am the real prize."

"I'm beginning to hate you a little, which is a shame because I had a real good fantasy going about you."

The corners of his mouth curve up, flirting with a real smile. My stomach does a loop-de-loop, and I suddenly can't remember why I was so mad I was ready to march out the door.

His eyes are dancing with good humor. "And am I naked in this fantasy?"

I shut my mouth, not wanting to dig myself a deeper

hole. The vibe has shifted to a shimmering heat. *You can't have him.*

His fingers trail lightly down my throat, and I swallow. "The virgin princess fantasizes about me."

"It was metaphorical."

His gaze is eating me up, dropping to my lips, my throat, my bare shoulder, back to my eyes. He's close but not touching me, heat radiating off him. "Was it?"

He wants to kiss me again, and God help me, I want it too. What is it about this man that makes me forget myself? I'm usually in much better control.

I babble on. "I mean, yes, you were naked, but I really think that's because I saw you that way, you know, in your bedroom briefs, not just for the bedroom, you probably have them on right now." I cough, really trying not to look down. "And the metaphor part is that I secretly wanted to expose you as a way of…getting to know you better." I'm breathless at the hot look in his eyes. "So we could be friends," I finish unconvincingly. "An alliance of kingdoms would be most…" I trail off; even I'm not buying it.

Lust or escape, fight or flight. I'm caught in the crosshairs of primal instincts more powerful than I've ever felt before because…Gabriel. He seems aware of every ounce of lust I'm trying desperately not to unleash. Maybe because he's equally in lust.

I take a deep breath and make one last attempt on Polly's behalf before I do the right thing and make my escape. "Your Highness, I strongly suggest you skip the spiders in favor of another athletic event. Maybe a triathlon." Like I could finish a triathlon. I don't know what I'm saying.

He lifts a hand and pulls a lock of my hair. "Springy." He strokes my hair, pushing it back over my shoulder, his fingers trailing lightly over my skin, drawing a hot shiver. "Call me Gabriel."

"Gabriel," I breathe. And then I run out of air because Gabriel Rourke is kissing me.

Our bodies slam together. We're wild, consuming each other, clawing at each other. Insanity. My world spins, and I clutch his shoulders, Gabriel my only anchor.

He breaks the kiss long minutes later, both of us breathing heavily, and shifts, kissing his way roughly down the side of my neck, his teeth scraping against me. I am on fire.

"I'm a virgin," I gasp out in a last desperate attempt to contain the fire.

He gives me a feral smile. "Then let me do what I normally do with virgins." He scoops me up, cradled in his arms, carrying me to the sofa.

"You do virgins a lot?"

He doesn't reply, merely sets me on my feet in front of the sofa and kisses me breathless again. His fingers expertly undo the back clasp and zip of my skirt, and it falls to my feet. He bites my lower lip gently before dropping to my feet and helping me step out of the skirt.

His gaze lifts, riveted on my leopard-print thong. What can I say? Leopards and I are simpatico. If they make it in leopard print, I want it.

"Racy for a virgin princess," he murmurs, already sliding the thong off me. I step out of that too. He's still fully dressed, and I like where this is going.

"No one would see my thong except my maid, and she understands me."

I'm not sure if he's buying it. Maybe he's as far gone as I am, because then he pushes me down to the sofa, grabs me by the hips, and pulls me to the edge. He kneels in front of me, his large warm hands sliding up my inner thighs, spreading my legs wide open.

His gaze meets mine, a moment's hesitation, his voice gravelly. "May I kiss you?"

"God, yes."

And then he kisses me softly right there, x marks the spot, and the princess wins a prize. *Fuck yes.* I grab him by the hair and moan. Even a virgin princess would moan in this situation, I reassure myself.

And then there's nothing but his hot hungry mouth expertly driving me up, up, up the heights I haven't seen in way too long. It goes on and on, my moans loud and lusty. I couldn't hold back if I wanted to. And then his fingers join the action, and I'm thrashing, overwhelmed. He clamps his hand on my hip, stilling me. The intensity ratchets up instantly, and I'm *gone.* I cry out as a monster orgasm rips through me, an explosion that leaves me trembling in the aftermath. He kisses my inner thigh and then nips it.

I laugh, giddy at the euphoric rush of pleasure. I hold his gorgeous face in both hands and give him a resounding kiss. "You rock, Gabriel Rourke."

He grins and it's like the sun comes out. He should always be this happy. I'm about to return the favor when it occurs to me the real Polly wouldn't know how to give a blow job and might even get serious flack for it. Her monarchy is old school.

"Show me how to pleasure you," I say instead.

He groans and slides my thong back on. "We'll work up to that."

"I'm ready and willing, Gabriel." I throw his name in there because I know he likes it. I don't think many people call him by his given name. I've heard a lot of *Your High-*

ness and *sir* around here. "And I'm not sure how much time I have left here. Please let me return the favor."

He meets my eyes for a moment, shakes his head, and then pulls my skirt back up. I stand and wiggle it over my hips. He turns me and does the zipper and clasp for me.

"No?" I'm shockingly disappointed.

He cups my ass with both his hands, giving me a squeeze. "I've already compromised you terribly. Keep this just between us, okay?"

"Okay."

He turns me back to him and kisses me roughly. I taste myself, and it's so erotic I try to climb his body. He pulls away before I can get a good foothold.

Then I'm looking at his retreating back without one word of goodbye after all we shared.

"See you at the triathlon," I call.

"Tarantulas at the finish line," he returns and then he's gone.

I shiver. They don't have tarantulas here, do they?

8

____

Anna

I belatedly remember Gabriel invited me to his room for dinner, and by late afternoon I'm actually nervous like this is a real date or something. I'm imagining dining by candlelight, intimate conversation as he finally drops the weight of being the crown prince and relaxes as just himself. At least I assume in the privacy of his suite he would be himself. He definitely seemed different last night when I showed up in his room with my plan to rescue both him and Polly. And he was divinely dirty in his private sitting room.

I'm standing in front of the closet, picking through my meager wardrobe for the perfect outfit that says sexy yet date appropriate, when there's a knock at the door.

"Come in," I call, turning to the door.

Anna steps inside and does a quick curtsy. "Your Highness, the crown prince sends his apologies that he won't be able to meet you for dinner tonight."

My happy bubble pops, and my shoulders droop, my

limbs suddenly heavy. "Oh." I straighten my spine and square my shoulders. "Did he say why?"

"No, ma'am."

I bob my head. My chest is tight like a big hand is pressing down on me. I tell myself I shouldn't feel hurt or disappointed. I was living in a dream world that I, Anna Hebert, was actually going to have a date with Gabriel, the crown prince. I turn back to the closet and shut the door. No need for the perfect outfit now.

Anna speaks again in a sympathetic voice. "I heard he left Villroy. Perhaps he had something he needed to attend to."

He left Villroy? My eyes well up, and I order them to knock it off. I've never been a big crier. "Did he say when he would return?"

"No, ma'am."

I turn to face her and give her a weak smile. "Thank you, Anna."

She bobs her head, curtsies, and walks swiftly out the door.

I cross to the bed and flop backward on it. I shouldn't be this upset. Except what if I never see him again? I never got to say goodbye or thank him for his generosity in giving me a spectacular orgasm and asking for nothing in return. Oh shit. What if that's the reason he left? He was trying to restrain himself from taking Polly's innocence. Is he hooking up with another woman to deal with his unsatisfied lust? My gut does a slow roll. I have no right to be jealous, no right to Gabriel at all, yet everything in me rebels at the thought of him with another woman.

And then it hits me. The terrible incredibly stupid truth—I'm falling for him.

I place the blame entirely on his magnificent shoulders.

With his smoldering looks and gruff tenderness, any woman would fall hard. And the worst part is, I know it's impossible. Even if he forgave me for lying about who I am, which is not at all a sure thing, he needs to marry nobility. Otherwise, why would we be having this competition among princesses? I'm the furthest thing from nobility—an American orphan—and I could never fit the traditional royal mold. My distant relation to Polly—sixth cousins tied by a common ancestor eight generations back —doesn't count as royal anything. She was clear on that. I'm still a commoner.

I sit up and swing my legs over the side of the bed. Enough wallowing. I came here with a specific goal. That's where I need to focus. I'll stick around until I win something of value, and then I'll take the money and run. I have to rescue Polly. That's all that matters.

Only what if the competition is over while Gabriel is gone?

I slept terribly and drag myself down to the parlor for breakfast. I should be happy because Anna told me this morning that the queen will join us at breakfast to give us further instructions, which means the competition will continue. Or it could mean the queen is going to choose a bride in Gabriel's absence and send the rest of us packing. I'm not sure what it means. I'm irritated, fatigued, and want to punch someone.

I get myself a cup of coffee, slather butter on toast, and slump into a seat. There are only six of us left on day three. The two princesses with backbones, Marguerite and Francesca, who I suggested as ideal matches for Gabriel, are still here. I'm insanely jealous of them both. If the competition keeps going, I just know one of them will win the ultimate prize. One of them will have what I can never have.

Today's competition, if there is one, will be my last. I tried my best, I really did, but I can't stay here when everything about this place reminds me of *him*.

I force down my toast and slurp my coffee, head down, stewing in silence while the princesses murmur to each other in polite conversation. After I finish, I lift my head, and one look at the pretty princesses sitting around the table sipping tea makes me think guiltily of Polly.

I exhale sharply. This is all Gabriel's fault. If he weren't such an irresistible temptation, I never would be in this horrible predicament. Damn you, Gabriel Rourke! I swear if I ever see you again, I will tear you—

"Gabriel!" I leap from my seat in my surprise.

He's walking behind the queen, but I can only focus on him. His piercing blue-green eyes lock on mine for an intense moment before he continues on to the head of the table.

The queen has her sour-lemon face on. The princesses are standing and shooting me sideways looks like I did the wrong thing again. Was it calling Gabriel by his given name instead of Your Highness? Or was it something with the queen? Crap. I forgot to bow my head and curtsy to the queen.

I do a belated head bow and curtsy to her. "Good morning, Your Majesty."

She says nothing, merely takes her seat at the head of the table. We all follow suit, except Gabriel, who remains standing.

The queen lifts a hand. "To make things interesting

and to remind you of the real prize, today one of you will win a diamond necklace worthy of a queen."

I suck in air. *Yes!* I catch Gabriel's eye. One side of his mouth curls up in a small smile that warms me to my toes. Maybe he wasn't hooking up with another woman last night. Maybe he had some charity event or royal duty to attend to. Maybe he was trying to keep the temptation of virgin Polly at bay all while arranging today's prize specifically to help me. Maybe he'll help me win it too. The tension drains from me, leaving me almost woozy. Maybe I'm halfway in love with him, which is stupid and wrong, but when he does amazing things like this, I can't help myself.

The queen goes on. "To win, you must each solve a puzzle. Each puzzle is different. The first one to solve their puzzle correctly will be given the location of the prize."

"A jigsaw puzzle, Your Majesty?" I ask.

Her lips form a disapproving slash. "All will be answered in due time." She gestures to the servants waiting nearby. The table is quickly cleared.

We all watch as another servant steps forward with a large open basket and neatly sets a piece of paper, pencil, and notepad in front of each princess. My heart sinks. It's not a jigsaw puzzle. I suck at brain teasers. My brain doesn't like to be teased; it likes to be satisfied with real-world questions and answers.

"I'll leave you to it," the queen says and stands. Everyone immediately stands, bowing and curtsying to her. She leaves and Gabriel follows, shooting me a sympathetic look before heading out. That can't be good.

I take my seat again. My paper says "home bias in trade puzzle" in bold at the top. My stomach drops as I read the instructions. It's a puzzle involving the clash of economic theory and practice. Uh, hello? They didn't cover advanced economics in beauty school. I glance over at Elizabeth's puzzle to my right. Hers says the Backus-Smith puzzle. This was definitely the twisted queen's idea. Gabriel would keep it easy, I think, something where he could give me an advantage and help me win. Plus he looked like he felt sorry for me having to do an economics puzzle.

I am so screwed. I casually flip through the notepad in case Gabriel left me a secret clue. Nothing. I glance around at the furrowed brows of the other princesses, hoping economics wasn't involved in their education either.

We're left alone to solve our puzzles with only one servant monitoring us, Albert, the old guy who unsuccessfully tried to teach the princesses how to ride bikes. The women are quiet, the only sound pencils scratching on paper. My pencil remains on the table because I don't even know where to start.

A long time passes. I'm not sure how long, but my ass is sore from sitting on the hard wooden chair for so long, and I'm getting PTSD flashbacks to high school, my hands clammy, my nerves on edge, knowing I'm going to get a big fat red F scrawled across my empty page. The worst part is it's not just me who failed today. I've failed Polly too. This was the kind of prize that would've made her freedom possible.

Suddenly Francesca leaps up and presents her puzzle to Albert. He gives her a small slip of paper, which she reads and then immediately runs from the room.

I leap up to follow her, and everyone else does too. Surely the queen saw this coming. There's one prize and Francesca is leading us right to it.

Francesca glances over her shoulder at the pack of

princesses at her back and picks up speed, barreling through a long hallway that leads to the courtyard. We're at a full run now. She dashes past manicured gardens and keeps going all the way to a small children's play area with a sandbox. She drops to her knees and starts digging with her hands. That's how badly she wants a diamond necklace. Dignified, composed Princess Francesca is digging in the sand. Well, guess what? I want it more.

I join her, digging all around, feeling for a box. Suddenly the six of us are crammed into the sandbox in a frenzy of digging. Sand is flying everywhere, elbows jabbing for space. We're savages, feral competitors desperate for the prize. Someone knocks into my shoulder hard, but I just keep going.

Out of the corner of my eye, I see Elizabeth lift a wooden box. We turn like a well-oiled predatory machine, all of us with our eyes on that box. I dive for it in near unison with the other women, caught in a tangle of arms and legs as we battle for possession. Elizabeth is losing her grip, only one hand on the box now. Before I can grab it, Francesca pulls Elizabeth's arm so hard she drops the box and lets out an unearthly scream like she's being murdered.

We freeze for a moment. Elizabeth's arm looks weird, hanging there at an odd angle. Suddenly she collapses in a dead faint from the pain.

"Help!" I holler, leaping out of the sandbox. "We need a doctor!" I'm not sure if her arm is broken or dislocated. It's probably better she's unconscious with that kind of pain.

Albert appears from behind the shrubbery. "I've got it." He pulls a phone from his pocket, urgently requests help, and then goes to Elizabeth's side.

Francesca has left the sandbox, the box in her possession now, but Marguerite is on her back, wildly clawing for the box from behind. The other princesses stand next to Elizabeth, staring down at her and whispering.

Elizabeth has the help she needs, so I waste no time and rush to the front of Francesca to snag the box. She's strong and puts up a good fight, but Marguerite is holding her back, and the box is mine. Yes!

I sprint back through the gardens, through the hallways of the palace, and straight upstairs to the safety of my room. I lock the door and barricade it with a chair jammed under the doorknob.

Finally, still breathing hard, my heart pounding, I open the box. Oh my God. It's beautiful—a chain of glittering diamonds with a huge diamond pendant hanging from the center. This should be in a museum. The pendant alone would be enough to do right by Polly. With shaking hands, I lift the necklace from the box and put it on. I gaze down at the beauty of it and go to the vanity mirror to admire it more, imagining just for a moment that I really am a princess and I'm about to attend a royal ball.

The doorknob rattles harshly, startling me. Someone raps hard on the door. "Security," a man's voice barks. "Open the door."

My heart leaps to my throat. Security is going to accuse me of stealing this necklace. It was all a setup to toss me in jail and throw away the key. The queen's revenge for all my impertinence.

"Be right there!" I quickly take off the necklace and put it back in its box. Then I stuff it in the back of the vanity drawer, hiding the evidence.

"We're breaking the door down!" the security man barks.

"I'll open it!" I race to the door, drag the chair away, and unlock it. I jump back just in time as the door flies open and four security guards swarm into the room followed by the queen and Gabriel.

Security scours the room, tossing about my meager wardrobe as they empty dresser drawers and go through the closet. One of the guards finds the box in the vanity drawer. "Got it," he says, and the team stands down.

Everyone watches as he opens the box and slams it shut. "It's all here, Your Majesty."

"Very well," the queen says. "See that it gets to Francesca. You may go." The security team leaves and she turns to me. "You didn't solve the puzzle. This was a test of the mind not of the body."

I hold my breath, waiting for the hammer to fall. What does the queen have against me? This prize wouldn't have meant I was the one chosen for Gabriel. There are still six of us here, still more competing to do. And, dammit, I *needed* this.

The queen stares at me for a long moment. "What do you have to say for yourself?"

I silently seethe at the accusation in her tone. I didn't do anything different than the other princesses. We were all grappling for the prize. I glance at Gabriel. He's quiet, but he doesn't look judgmental.

I address the queen in a civil tone. "Your Majesty, I haven't been taught economic theory. Ask me anything practical and I could tell you a solution."

"She used her wits to best the others," Gabriel puts in, coming to my defense. It's not true. I used my fighting instincts honed on years of defending myself from foster home bullies. He wants me to win. Does he actually want me for his wife now? The thought simultaneously elates me and terrifies me. He doesn't know the real me. He doesn't know it's impossible.

The queen harrumphs. "She yanked the prize from the true winner like a playground bully."

Gabriel fires back, "What about Francesca? She pulled Elizabeth's shoulder right out of its socket. And Polly was the only one who stopped grappling for the prize to call for a doctor."

The queen grimaces. "That was unfortunate. Marguerite lost a tooth too." She slowly shakes her head before saying, "This didn't go the way I envisioned. We will correct and carry on." She leaves.

Gabriel mouths *sorry* to me and follows her out the door.

He's on my side now. Somehow that means so much more than a diamond necklace. Tonight I'll go to his room, and together we'll make a plan to end this crazy competition to both of our benefits. If not, I'll have to say goodbye.

My gut churns, my chest tight. Maybe goodbye is the only option. A future with Gabriel is a royal fantasy, and haven't all of those been shattered?

9

____

Gabriel

I stare at the ceiling in my empty bed, wide-awake, stupidly hoping Polly will join me here. I'm torturing myself because I know I shouldn't go after a virgin. If she comes to me on her own, then it would mean she wants this as much as I do, and I'd have nothing to feel guilty about. I want her badly, even knowing it cannot go any further. I can't ask her to be my wife and destroy her spirit with the traditional kind of life she's turned her back on in her own kingdom. Not to mention the fact that my mother has taken an intense dislike to her. She called frigging security on her!

I scrub a hand over my face. I had to leave Villroy entirely last night to avoid the temptation of Polly. I met up with one of my usual lovers in Paris for dinner, and that was where it ended. I couldn't go through with it. Suddenly, beautiful sophisticated Katrina seemed too quiet, too coy, her blond hair too thin and lacking in curls. I wanted her to be Polly.

I headed straight home, formulating a plan. I thought

if I set up today's competition so that Polly could easily win a prize of some value, she'd be so overcome with gratitude for my help that we'd share a night together before she left. Yup. Thinking with my dick with predictably poor results.

It was my idea to offer the necklace. The economic puzzles were not. I can't figure out what my mother was thinking with that one. Of course it would come down to a brawl with the puzzle winner leading the way to the prize. Was that always the goal? Maybe she thought a catfight would be entertaining. She probably didn't anticipate it would get out of hand with real injuries. In fact, the two wounded princesses, Elizabeth and Marguerite, left on their own, fed up with the whole barbaric game, and who could blame them? I watched the brawl on the closed-circuit TV, rooting for Polly the whole time. And my girl won.

Not my girl. The fact that the prize was taken from her can only mean this game is rigged against her. Not surprising since my mother has been clear that Polly is not suited to be queen.

I roll to my side and stare at the bedroom door, willing her to appear. Long moments pass and my hope fades. I close my eyes, my mind flashing back to my time with Polly. When she first walked into the palace in her loud sexy dress and mistook me for the butler. Outrageous.

Polly in a bikini, unknowingly giving me a sexy show. Tempting.

Polly hugging me as we shared our pain. Deeply touching.

Polly sneaking into my room to barter a deal with me. Kissing her, touching her, tasting her. I veer away from that memory, already aching with need.

The dark of the cave when I startled her, and she hugged me tight like I was a comfort. I've never been anyone's comfort.

My eyes fly open at the creak of the bedroom door. The outline of wild curls and a short robe have me reaching out in the dark. She closes the door and pads slowly in. I realize she can't see me, and I turn on the light on the nightstand.

She smiles. My chest expands with a surge of affection. Somehow it's like she really sees me and not all the royal trappings that keep others at a distance. I'm absurdly happy she's here.

She slips out of her sandals and stands next to the bed, looking down at me. "You're awake."

"What took you so long?" I pull her into bed with me and turn off the light.

"You were expecting me?" she whispers, cuddling right up against me. I'm in my boxer briefs, and the feel of warm sexy woman against my bare skin is exquisite sensual torture.

I cup her jaw and lift her face for my kiss. "Yes." I slide my leg between hers, and we lie there, sideways hugging as close as two people can be while keeping one a virgin.

"This competition has gotten out of hand," she whispers.

I keep my voice low. "Agreed. And you should've won today." I don't know why, but lying in the dark whispering feels more intimate than anything physical.

Her fingers slide through the hair at the nape of my neck. "The queen doesn't like me."

I rub her back, trying to soothe. "It's not personal. She wants the best candidate for the job of queen. She knows what it takes."

"And she thinks I don't have what it takes."

I smooth her hair back from her face, enjoying the soft curls. "I have a feeling my mother has her ideal candidate in mind already."

"Francesca."

"Maybe, I'm not sure. I just know it's not you."

Silence. Maybe I hurt her feelings.

I give her a small squeeze. "This competition is the last thing I wanted, but it brings my father comfort."

She's quiet for a moment. "I haven't seen him. Are there hidden cameras so he can watch?"

I wince because that sounds creepy, but there are extenuating circumstances—his poor health, the need for a smooth succession, the future of the kingdom. "Yes. He's very ill, bedridden for the better part of a year. He watches on closed-circuit TV."

"I thought so." She stiffens. "Is there one in here?"

"No, only where the princesses are taken for meals and competitions." I hesitate, but then I find I really want to share. "Can I trust you with something very few people know?"

"Yes. Cross my heart and spit in your eye."

I find myself smiling in the dark. She's outrageous and fun, something I haven't had much of in my life.

"Is it about your dad?" she whispers. "Is it bad?"

I stop smiling. "Yes. He has late-stage pancreatic cancer. The doctors say there's not much time left for him. This competition is not the usual thing for my parents. They're normally the height of royal decorum. It's the cancer that brought them to this point, seeking joy in any small way they can."

"I get that." She hugs me tight. "I'm so sorry, Gabriel. I know how hard it is. My dad was sent home to die. It's awful losing someone you love, day by day, and being helpless to do anything about it."

I hold her close and let out a breath. She understands. Suddenly I don't feel so alone with my hidden pain.

I find myself sharing more. "My mother refuses to rule without him. That's why there's an urgency to securing the line of succession. I must marry a woman ready to step in as queen and produce the next heir to the throne."

She strokes a hand down my back. "Why is there so much pressure on you? What about Phillip? Don't you have other siblings too?"

"I have four younger brothers and two younger sisters, but none of them are suitable. They haven't been groomed for this from birth. My indulgent father let them run wild the way he did as the younger sibling. He had to unexpectedly become king when his older brother married a commoner and abdicated the throne. It was quite a scandal—never been done before in the history of the kingdom—and very hard for my father to adjust from his carefree life to the rigor of being king. He's always wanted my younger siblings to have the freedom he was denied."

"Wow. That must've been true love for your uncle to give up the throne."

"I suppose, but not without its consequences. He's been banned from Villroy, and his family has been cut off. No funds, no privileges. My father calls them the riffraff."

"Harsh."

I rest my chin on top of her head. "Sometimes life is."

She pulls back and speaks fiercely. "This whole thing is unfair to you. Your parents put all the pressure on you to lead. They took away your freedom."

I love that she rises to my defense, even if it's unnecessary. I play with a lock of her hair. "They knew I was up to the task. It's not a hardship. I've always been proud of my birthright and know my place."

"I still don't think it's right that your parents didn't give you the same freedoms as your siblings, or at least make a few of them learn the ropes too. That's why you're so grim."

"I'm not grim."

She's stroking me now, her hand skimming over my shoulder and down my back. "Did they lock you in the attic and force you to learn with endless tutors?"

I let out a breath. "I wasn't locked away, but my education and training were different. My siblings are unprepared to step into the role. Maybe part of me liked being the big brother and shielding them from the rigors of doing one's duty, though one of my younger sisters has made a few concessions to duty."

Her fingers trail back to my shoulder and down to my bicep, which she squeezes. "Damn, seven kids. Your parents got busy between the sheets, didn't they?"

I chuckle. "The two youngest are twins, a boy and a girl. That's Silvia and Adrian. My mother wanted a daughter so badly after four sons in a row. That's when she had Emma. And then she wanted Emma to have a sister, so she tried again. And it worked. She just didn't expect her sixth kid to be six and seven."

"Talk about a surprise."

We're quiet for a few moments, just holding each other in the dark. I'm content, a rare feeling for me.

"Gabriel."

I love the sound of my name on her lips. "Yes?"

"I came here tonight to say goodbye. It's clear I won't be allowed to win the competition, not even a smaller prize like a diamond necklace. You being the grand prize."

I tighten my arms around her, not ready to say good-bye. "So you admit I'm the big reward?"

She laughs. "You're on your own plane of greatness, way, way up there, but don't let it go to your head, Your Highness." I can hear the good humor in her voice, but then she becomes serious. "I'm sorry, but if there's nothing for me to take home of value, I have to go and find another way."

"Tell me why you need the funds. Who is this person you're helping and why?"

Her fingers flex on my arm. "I'm not supposed to say."

"You can trust me, Polly. I swear on my life."

She speaks in a rush of words. "All I can say is she's in trouble and it's urgent that I help her. Very time sensitive. She's important to our kingdom."

"Why can't your kingdom help her? I thought your economy was thriving."

"It's a delicate situation that can't be taken care of through royal channels. There's just me trying to make it right. I swear my intentions are good. I'm only doing what I have to do."

Like me, she does what she needs to do for the good of her kingdom. Duty, honor, obligation. These I understand; these I value immensely. The walls I've always kept around my heart crumble as I finally admit the truth to myself—I'm in love with her. It's too fast, crazy even, yet I'm strangely unconcerned. I'm lit up inside, alive and aware, completely tuned in to the sheer joy of holding her. The heat of her body through the silky robe, her spicy floral scent, the soft smooth skin of her legs pressed against mine. My God, I'm actually happy.

I kiss her tenderly. "I'll help you. Tomorrow's prize will be something of value that cannot be taken from you, only used for the good of your kingdom." I could give her a jewel right now, but I selfishly want to keep her here as long as possible. Our monarchy has wealth in the form of jewels and some well-placed investments—we're far from destitute—but that's not enough to save our economy. Villroy must be self-sustaining to support generations to come.

"Thank you." She's quiet for a moment. "There will be only two of us left after tomorrow, so then I guess…after I leave, you'll marry whoever is left."

I want to marry *her*. I want my happiness over hers and that is not honorable. I cannot go against my parents' wishes while my father is near death. He will side with my mother against Polly. I cannot ask Polly to squash her free spirit and confine herself to the restrictions of the royal life of a queen, especially with the additional burden of our faltering economy. Or can I?

"Do you miss home?" I ask.

She doesn't answer. Maybe it's a sore subject.

"I ask because you seem different from your pictures at official events. More free and outgoing now."

"You looked me up?"

"Yes. I was curious."

She's quiet for so long I think she won't answer, but she finally says, "I don't miss home. It was stifling. I needed to get away and experience freedom. But that doesn't mean I won't do right by them."

"I understand." It's as I suspected. She would not be happy with the rigors required of the queen here in Villroy.

She sighs. "Thank you for understanding and for helping me."

There's nothing more to say. We have only this, and I

can't deny myself any longer. I roll on top of her and kiss her. The pleasure of my body finally fully pressed against hers is staggering. She returns my passion, eager, enthusiastic, and I tell myself that nothing that happens between us can be wrong.

~

Anna

This is our last night together. He'll give me what I need to help Polly. I can never be what he needs as a wife, a queen. I'm just the kind of commoner they'd toss out on their ass—an orphan. I tell myself it doesn't matter what I do now. I can be me in the dark privacy of Gabriel's room. We both understand what this is.

He's gentle with me, so gentle as he pushes me to my back and kisses me. Slow deep kisses, his hands smoothly stroking over my robe, down my arms, my sides, my legs. It's decadent, and I melt into the mattress. He lifts his head and leans back just enough to untie my robe. I'm wearing a black cotton V-neck slip. I sit up and take off everything—robe, slip, thong—and fling them to the far side of the king-size bed. Ha! King-size for a future king. But he's not a king to me when it's the two of us. He's just Gabriel.

He turns on the bedside lamp, and I blink against the sudden brightness. "I needed to see you." His voice is gravelly. "You're beautiful, so beautiful."

"Thank you." I look my fill at his gorgeous muscular shoulders, wide chest, flat abs, and hard cock straining against his boxer briefs. "So are you."

He cradles my face with both hands and kisses me deeply, and then he's guiding me back to the mattress, his body covering mine. He holds himself up on his forearms, holding most of his weight as he kisses his way across my jaw to the sensitive spot under my ear, letting his teeth scrape there, drawing a hot shiver before continuing down my throat, my collarbone, and then lavishing attention on my breasts, kissing and tasting like he has all the time in the world.

I have never been treated this way in bed. Like I'm precious, a jewel that he wants to discover. I'm warm and languid, relaxed with a man in a way that's foreign to me. Like we were always meant to come together in this way.

I sink my fingers into his thick hair and give a tug, urging him back for a kiss. He returns to my mouth, and I kiss him passionately. His hand slides up my ribs to my breast, his fingers pinching my nipple. The sharp sensation steals my breath. He shifts downward again, taking my hard nipple into his mouth and suckling. My back arches, each hard suck bringing a delicious tightening inside me.

I spread my legs wide in invitation, needing him there. He seems to understand without a word from me as he shifts to my other breast, suckling hard, his hand trailing down my belly and between my legs. Even then, he's in no rush, teasing me lightly with his fingers.

I lift my hips. "More."

He gives me a wicked smile before giving me a pinch that's an electric shock. I cry out and then he lowers his head, his tongue soothing, licking across my tight bud. White-hot jolts of pleasure rock me with every lap of his tongue. *Fu-u-uck.* I grip his hair, moaning loudly.

I never want him to stop. Never, ever.

My mind shuts down, my fingers loosening their grip as I float in a haze of pleasure. His mouth is hungry, and then he slides a finger inside me and then another. I moan softly.

He lifts his head, and, worse, he withdraws his fingers, resting them on my upper thigh. "Polly, I don't mean to be indelicate, but you don't feel like a virgin. You can be honest with me."

Think, Anna! My brain scrambles for an explanation other than I lost it in Joey's Subaru after prom. I can't fuck this up. This is my one and only chance to be with him. My gut tells me this is not the time to blurt out one hundred percent truth. I want him so desperately. *Think!* Tampon, maybe, definitely TMI, or maybe gymnastics or horseback riding. I don't know! I just need him back *now.* "Sometimes there's no hymen or, um, other things can happen to it. Womanly things."

"Ah."

I grip his hair with one hand, trying to pull him back where he belongs, pleasuring me, because I am a horny desperate liar.

I'm going to hell.

I don't care.

His mouth resumes its magic. My hips arch up to meet him, electric sensations rushing through me. On and on and on. I'm lost once again in a haze of pleasure, blissfully riding the wave. His fingers are back, sliding deep inside me, stroking me and then…*yes!* G-spot triggered, my hips buck wildly. I'm hurtling toward a monster orgasm when he lifts his head and withdraws his fingers. *No-o-o-o!*

"Don't stop!" I bark.

"Do you pleasure yourself?"

"I'm a twenty-three-year-old virgin," I snap. "What do you think?"

"Show me."

I comply because I'm so freaking close I want to scream, and if he's just going to dick around…He watches me, licking his lips. It's not as good with my fingers. I need him. "Gabriel, please, I want your mouth on me so badly. Please, please, please." I'm begging shamelessly because he's that good.

"I want to watch more. Show me what you like."

I jackknife upright. "You like to live dangerously, huh?"

He gives me a shove, pushing me flat on my back. "Do as I say; then you'll receive."

I'm furious he's leaving me hanging like this. And he's much too bossy. I glare at him as my fingers trail down and circle the way I like.

"Good girl," he croons, making me wetter.

I close my eyes, trying to get the deep pleasure back. I feel him moving and then the mattress shifts as he lies next to me, his voice husky in my ear, urging me on with his filthy talk. I'm seriously pissed off and seriously turned on. And—

"Oh, oh, oh." My breath hitches. He shoves my hand away and then his glorious mouth is back, carrying me up, up, up, higher and higher. I break violently, my body shuddering with it, the sensation radiating out to the top of my tingling scalp to the tips of my toes.

"Gabriel," I sigh when I can speak again.

He climbs up my body and kisses me. "Glad to be of service."

"You should be knighted for that. Next time don't stop or I will strangle you with my bare hands."

He's quiet, serious as he looks down at me, and I realize there is no next time. I ignore the dull ache of regret in my chest and force myself to focus on the here and now.

His fingers slide between my legs, cupping me, and I moan long and low. Is next time now? I'm not sure if I can come again so soon. He shifts, taking my nipple deep in his mouth. I spread my legs wider and moan softly, the ache inside me needing to be filled.

He takes the hint, and his fingers slide inside me. It turns out I can take more because I'm greedy for him. And when his lips kiss a hot trail down my stomach, my belly dips, my womb aches, and all of me tightens in anticipation. He is *the* man. Twice in one night, I can hardly believe it. Maybe it's because he thinks I'm a virgin, so he needs to get me really hot, and I'm definitely going to hell, but I will die happy. He positions himself kneeling between my legs, his hands sliding up the inside of my thighs, spreading them further, and then finally his mouth closes over my sex. *Yes! Yes! Yes!*

His lips vibrate against me in a low chuckle that brings more pleasure. Did I say that out loud? My brain goes dark as he consumes me. I grab onto his big shoulders, my nails digging in as he works me with his lips and tongue and teeth. *Fuck me. I'm on fire.* His fingers join the action, stroking me on the inside as he starts to suck gently. My body jerks and then I'm flying, a harsh cry ripped from my throat as I rock helplessly against him. He gentles, bringing me back to earth, slow warm waves of pleasure rippling through me. I'm glowing inside and out.

"I worship you," I blurt.

He flashes a smile and climbs up my body, gazing warmly down at me with a look that almost feels like love. My jaw goes slack. I'm stunned, stupid happy between the orgasms and Gabriel's loving look.

He kisses me and then he shifts, rolling me to my stomach, sliding my hair to the side and placing a soft kiss on the nape of my neck. I melt into the mattress, and then I jolt as sharp teeth sink into my nape in a light firm hold. My breath catches, a shiver of excitement running through me. He releases his hold, his hands roaming, followed by his hot mouth kissing and tasting from the nape of my neck down to my toes. There isn't one inch of me he hasn't kissed, touched, and tasted.

He rolls me back over to face him, a question in his eyes. I belatedly panic that I've been too loud, enjoying all this too much for a supposed virgin, but then I realize he's waiting, silently asking if he can take my virginity. A surge of affection rushes through me. He is the sweetest. That makes me wonder what he would've been like if he knew I wasn't a virgin. More aggressive? I'd be into that. I wish I could find out.

I wrap my arms around his neck. "I want you. Let's enjoy each other tonight. No one has to know."

He strokes his thumb across my lower lip. "Are you sure? Be sure."

I reach down and rub him through his boxer briefs. He's huge and rock hard. "I'm sure," I croak.

He smiles and my breath catches at the beauty of it. I wish I could always make him smile. "God, Polly, you've made me so happy."

"So now we can both be happy. Well, I can be happier. I'm already happy thanks to you."

He reaches into the nightstand drawer for a condom and rips it open. I helpfully pull off his boxer briefs, dropping a kiss on his massive erection. He groans. Then I can't help but taste, licking the length of him.

He grips my hair and lifts my head. "I want to be inside you."

"I want that too. I want everything. Let's stay up all night and do everything there is to do to each other."

He groans and rolls on the condom. Then he's on top of me, his hand cradling my face, gazing into my eyes as he fits himself to me. I wrap my legs high around his waist. Slowly he pushes inside. I'm no virgin, but it's been a while and he's thick. I can feel my body stretching, the ache as he pushes deeper.

His expression is fierce determination as he moves ever so slowly. Drops of sweat form on his forehead. He's straining to make it easier for the woman he thinks is a virgin. Tears sting my eyes, surprising me. I'm not a crier.

He stills. "Am I hurting you?"

I shake my head and look to the ceiling, hoping the tears will go back where they came from.

He starts to pull out, and I grab his ass and pull him hard against me. He slides in to the hilt, and we both moan. He kisses my eyelids, my cheeks, my jaw. My throat is nearly closed with emotion. What is wrong with me? I should be enjoying myself, along for a fun ride.

I buck under him. "You've got to move to make this work."

He chuckles and the soft exhalation of air tickles my ear. "I know how it works, darling."

The darling spears my heart. My breath shudders out as I crash into the hard truth—I'm one hundred percent all in, idiotically in love. My eyes are hot. I close them and swallow the lump of emotion lodged in my throat.

My breath catches on a sharp inhale as he thrusts deep. "Yes," I manage, needing him to take me back to the world of pleasure, away from the emotional abyss. *Fuck me hard.* I quickly change it to, "I love this so much. More, more, more."

He groans, his mouth slamming over mine as he thrusts into me. He lifts his head, his breath harsh by my ear as he takes me on a ride. It's not fun like my usual casual hookups; it's intense. Rough and hard and deep. Every stroke brings me closer to the edge.

"Come with me," he orders.

"You can't just demand—ah!" He has my ankle over his shoulder, and then he's kneeling, pumping into me even deeper than before. His fingers stroke me rapidly. I'm fever hot, panting, out of my mind. He's pushing me open with his hard thrusts as I tighten around him at the same time. I'm caught in the vortex of Gabriel pleasure, exquisite, nearly unbearable in its intensity. Pulsing hot pleasure rushes through me, and then I explode, crying out his name. That sets him off, pounding into me as he lets go.

I am shaking, sweating, high on Gabriel. I never want this night to end. More fucking. More everything.

He turns his head and kisses my calf. My tears spring back with a vengeance, leaking out of my eyes. I throw an arm over my eyes, thoroughly embarrassed.

He sets my leg down. "Polly, are you okay?"

I can't speak. If I do, I'll blurt out everything and it'll all end. He'll hate me for lying to him.

A moment later, he's next to me. He pushes my arm off my eyes and pulls me into his arms, lying side by side. My tears are wetting his chest, but he doesn't seem to mind. I throw an arm and a leg over him, plastering myself against him, knowing our time together is running out.

He strokes my hair, murmuring, "It's just between us, I

promise." He thinks I'm upset about losing my virginity, and his concern just makes me cry more.

"I know," I choke out. "I don't regret it. I loved it." *I love you.*

He holds me tight. "Okay. It'll be okay."

Except how can anything ever be okay again? I'm in love with the crown prince of Villroy, and he's going to marry another woman.

10

———

Gabriel

I've kept my word. I will help Polly win and send her home with the funds needed to help her friend. It pains me to know she's leaving, yet some part of me has hope. Our connection is too strong to ignore. We kept each other up most of the night, entwined together as close as two people could be. She took to my demands beautifully, satisfied me deeply, and even had a few demands of her own. She's fiery, passionate, and strong. I woke at dawn, content with Polly in my arms, knowing I couldn't let her go. We fit in a way no one has ever fit with me before. I don't know how it will work yet. All I know is I must find a way to keep her.

I made my suggestions to my mother for today's competition. Most of my input was ignored, but the part I really cared about, the prize, is all set. It will be a donation from our charitable foundation to her foundation. Polly can direct the funds from there. The value she named was much less than the value of the diamond necklace that was taken from her, though I suppose more than she could've managed on her own without drawing suspicion.

I'd hoped for a running or swimming event today, which she'd win handily. What I got was a test of strength and perseverance pulled straight from the reality show my parents love—four princesses on the beach, each struggling to get to the top of a greased pole to grab a flag.

I watch nearby, along with the servants chosen to oversee the competition. My parents are watching in their bedroom. After a princess gets her flag, she has to jump into a kayak and race to the north shore. The servants stand at the ready to push the kayaks off. None of them are burly men. In fact, Albert is old. I'm here ostensibly as judge, but I'm just waiting to step in and push Polly's kayak with all my strength to give her a head start.

I can practically hear my parents cackling with glee over the greased princesses. They're all wearing short-sleeved collared shirts with capris in a variety of pastels now ruined by large splotches of black grease. Except for Polly, who wears an inappropriate sexy-as-fuck halter top with short shorts. Even with the sexy outfit, I can barely watch her without cringing because she sucks at this.

I turn my attention to the other princesses. Francesca digs her fingernails into the pole and grips it with her bare feet. She's hanging on, but not moving up.

Sophia scrambles like a monkey, slips, and drops all the way to the ground. The sand sticks to her grease and sweat. I'm thinking the sand might help her with traction, but after trying to rub it off, she runs to the water and rinses all the sand away. Poor choice. Now she's too wet to make headway with the grease. I watch her first attempt as she grunts her way up and squeals her way down, rather like a pig.

Lucienne, who's been quietly close to the lead in every competition, but never winning, is experimentally trying different ways to climb. She leaps and slides without success. Next she digs her feet in at the bottom and pulls with her arms, sliding down after any progress gained. Finally, she successfully climbs hand over hand, her feet mimicking the motion. She's gaining some headway.

Polly slides down the pole for the third time and glares at it. "What?" she hollers at the pole. "Tell me how to climb you!" She kicks sand at it in frustration and then seems to think this is a good idea. She tosses big handfuls of sand at the pole. This time when she climbs, she's making progress.

"Ouch, ouch, ouch," she mutters. "Stupid pole. I will conquer you." The sand on this part of the island is coarse and must be digging into her palms and bare feet.

Go, Polly, go.

Francesca drops to the ground and dips her hands in the sand, starting over with better traction. Not a peep out of her over the coarse sand. She grimaces as she slowly makes progress.

Sophia slides to the bottom again. Now it's a pretty close race between Francesca, Lucienne, and Polly.

Lucienne makes it first, grabs the flag, slides back down the pole, and waves it around with a victory whoop. Wasting time.

Francesca grabs her flag and jumps to the ground, landing in a crouch and then taking off for a kayak. Lucienne does too.

I stay where I am, waiting for my girl. After last night, she is mine.

Sophia shakes her pole from the bottom, trying to

dislodge the flag, giving up on climbing it. She's out. Not following the rules disqualifies you.

Polly makes a huge reach and grabs her flag, sliding down the pole and sprinting to a kayak. I follow at a run. Albert is making his way toward her when I cut him off. "I'll do it."

She's fast, getting to the kayak a few seconds after the other two women. She grabs the paddle and digs in. I put my shoulder into it and give her kayak a mighty shove. She sails past the other two women.

"No fair!" Sophia shouts from shore, the sore loser. "Polly got a much bigger push than anyone else."

Francesca and Lucienne turn back to see me still knee-deep in the water behind Polly's kayak and exchange a look. Uh-oh. They must know I favor Polly. This is the first time I've intervened in a competition.

I turn back to shore and join the servants on a walk along the high cliff trail, following the kayak race from above. Polly is in the lead, but Francesca is gaining with powerful strokes.

A few moments later, Francesca rams the back of Polly's kayak. Polly's body jerks, but she doesn't capsize, and she manages to hang onto her paddle. She shouts something over her shoulder at Francesca, not seeing Lucienne coming up her other side. It's like watching a car crash. I can't look away.

Lucienne uses her paddle crosswise to give Polly a sideways shove and accidentally tips her own kayak, half falling onto Polly's kayak, which makes Polly's kayak tip precariously. Polly uses her paddle to shove Lucienne's kayak off and then paddles furiously away. Lucienne struggles to keep her kayak upright, losing valuable time.

Now it's Polly and Francesca in a tight race, Francesca

gaining on her. The wind picks up, helping their progress. Polly's curls are blowing all over the place like jagged wild flames. It reminds me of her, spirited and free, and I love it. Suddenly I don't want Polly to win. If she wins, she'll leave. If she's second place, I can have another night with her. Otherwise, I don't know how long I'll have to wait. I don't even know if I can convince her to keep seeing me, given the circumstances.

But I do know how to distract her. She's commented on it often enough.

I rip off my shirt, peer down at the rowing princesses, and holler, "Go, go, go!"

Polly looks up and beams a smile that hits me in the solar plexus. I'm momentarily breathless. "Right on, handsome!"

The servants stare at me with wide eyes. Not one word about my uncharacteristic spontaneity.

Francesca doesn't miss a beat, rowing faster. Lucienne, in third place, slows her efforts as Francesca pulls ahead. Neither of them looked up at my cheer.

Polly is behind now, as I'd hoped. I know it's selfish, but I also know she was tuned in to my voice and Francesca wasn't. Not that Francesca did anything wrong. Clearly the woman has great focus, strength, and perseverance. It's every quality a queen should have.

But it's Polly who makes me feel alive.

~

Anna

I'm paddling so hard my arms are burning from the exertion, especially after the greased-pole climb. Once again I'm distracted by man candy. Damn you, Gabriel, and your magnificent chest! Now Francesca is in the lead. I should've kept focused like Francesca the rowing machine over here. I swear she must row in her spare time. She's unbelievably precise in her strokes. I have to win. I briefly consider ramming Francesca's kayak, after all, she rammed mine, but that's not me. I don't take cheap shots. I give all I have, and if that's not enough, then I pivot to the next opportunity.

I ignore my screaming arm muscles, the strain in my back, and put my last ounce of energy into the race. We're nearly side by side, coming into the last stretch to the north shore, where a red banner between two poles on the beach indicates the finish line.

A wave sneaks up on us, lifting us and pushing us to shore. I paddle to stay ahead of it. Francesca stops paddling, letting the wave crash into her, probably hoping for some added momentum. I make it to the shallows, but she doesn't. Her kayak capsizes.

I get out of my kayak, drag it to shore, and burst through the finish line.

"Polly wins. Francesca is runner-up," Albert declares. "You both made it to the final round."

Francesca is standing in the shallows now, soaked, struggling to right her kayak. The staff goes to help her. She's furious and stomps to shore, not bothering to thank them for their help. I want to tell her not to worry, she'll win in the end. I just needed this prize to help out a princess back home, and then I'm out of here. She'll win the ultimate prize—Gabriel. I ignore the twist in my gut at the thought.

Like a sixth sense, I turn just as he reaches my side.

"You won," he says flatly.

Somehow I know how he feels. I should be leaping up

and down, whooping it up, but looking into his beautiful blue-green eyes the color of the sea, remembering what we shared, I don't feel so much like cheering. Now I'm supposed to take the money and run, never to see him again. "Yeah."

"Fair and square."

"You did give me a boost."

"Everyone had a boost."

I lower my voice. "Not everyone had a boost with a muscle man."

He smiles, and my heart thumps harder. His rare smiles are lethal. He dips his head and whispers directly in my ear, "Stay the weekend."

I nod. I don't have to think twice. It's not like a lawyer can do anything for Polly on the weekend anyway.

He smiles widely and then seems to remember the small audience of staff members nearby and returns to a neutral expression.

Francesca joins us. "Your Highness, this was a tough challenge. I'm happy to be in the final two, even if I didn't take first prize."

Gabriel inclines his head. "You'll both meet the family on Saturday at dinner, on Sunday you'll meet with the queen, and on Monday one of you will return home and one of you will remain at the palace for two weeks. This will give us time to get to know each other before the official engagement notice is posted." He meets my eyes, looks like he wants to say something more, and then changes his mind. He gives us both a small smile, turns, and walks away.

Francesca glares at me before stalking off to her waiting maid.

On Monday it will be Francesca who stays behind to

live happily ever after with her prince. I try to reconcile myself to this reality, torturing myself as I picture their two weeks of couple time on Villroy—a shiny paradise-like time on this beautiful island—and then the big royal announcement. I stop there out of self-preservation.

Now I know why we had to commit to three weeks at the palace. I suddenly realize the weekend invitation Gabriel whispered in my ear wasn't as intimate as I'd thought. But can I say no to him?

I stupidly fell in love. How did this happen? I've only been here for five days, yet there's no denying the intensity of all I'm feeling. Maybe it was the stress of the competition, the time we spent just the two of us. Maybe it was just Gabriel and his gruff tender ways. The way I knew instinctively that he needed me. And maybe I needed him too. I've never met a man like him, strong, proud, but also capable of great care and affection. He treated me like a precious jewel.

No one has ever treated me like a jewel. Because I'm not. I'm a scrappy, tough, lying beautician from Tampa, who got in over her head.

And now I have to do the most difficult thing of my life—let Gabriel go.

11

Gabriel

I spent last night with Polly, surprising her by seeking her out in her room when she didn't come to mine. I knew it was wrong to show up there with Francesca right down the hall, but I couldn't help myself. I can't appear to be playing favorites, especially after giving Polly's kayak a boost in today's competition. Polly confessed she didn't come to my room because she was trying to let me go. One kiss was all it took to remind us both of our intense connection.

I wish she was by my side tonight. My father has taken a turn for the worse, and I'm back in that dark place of despair. I know Polly would be a comfort, and I also know she wouldn't be welcome in his private suite. A doctor is attending to him now, making him more comfortable with pain medicine. I'm not ready to lose him, and I know it will devastate my mother. They're a team. I fear she'll lose the will to live without him, just as she has lost the desire to lead without him. All I really want is to make him better.

I arrive at my parents' suite, and I'm quickly ushered into the sitting room. My mother stands by my father's bedside, asking the doctor questions.

I pace the room. I never thought I'd actually want the barbaric bridal games to continue, but here it is six days later, and I'm sad that it's over because I'll have to say goodbye to Polly. Francesca defaults to my bride in Polly's absence. I asked Polly to stay the weekend to postpone the inevitable. I'm fooling myself, buying time.

Finally, the doctor leaves and I go to my father. "How are you feeling?"

His smile is more of a grimace. "I'll be fine once the pain meds kick in."

My mother squeezes his hand, her expression grim. "Rest, love." She takes her seat by his side.

I pull a chair over and sit next to her, all of us silent for a few minutes. My siblings arrive tomorrow. For the first time I fear my father might only have hours instead of days or weeks. I shouldn't have protected my brothers and sisters from this harsh reality. I'll never forgive myself if they don't have a chance to say goodbye. Thankfully, his expression relaxes as the medicine kicks in, and he goes right back to his favorite topic.

"It's down to two candidates," he says to me. "Your mother and I are in agreement. Francesca is the best choice."

My mother chimes in. "She was always our first choice, and I've made sure the competitions were suited to her. She has the largest wealthiest kingdom, and an alliance with her country will put us in the best position going forward. She's also right for the role of queen, raised in the proper fashion."

The unspoken words *and Polly is not right* are clear as

day. Something in me rebels for the first time in my life. I'm indifferent to Francesca, and before I met Polly, that wouldn't have bothered me in the least. I have only to look at the love my parents share to know I want that in my marriage too.

"So you rigged the games to favor Francesca?" I ask.

My mother replies without an ounce of remorse. "Yes."

I narrow my eyes. "Why not just choose her and be done with it?"

She gives me a sad smile. "Your father needed something to look forward to."

"I've enjoyed it immensely," my father says before launching into a coughing fit. My mother helps him with a sip of water.

It's as simple and twisted as that. A small sliver of joy in his suffering. This was the only reason I went along with the competition in the first place, though I don't think I would've bothered if I'd known it was rigged. But then I wouldn't have gotten to know Polly. I can't work up much anger for their rigged game because Polly brought me great happiness, comfort, and, yes, love.

After he's settled back again, I speak up. "I'm not sure about Francesca. Maybe we can delay, put out some more feelers through royal channels." I need time to work something out with Polly.

My father's voice is hoarse. "End the games. Make the right choice, Gabriel." His eyes drift closed. "Running out of time," he murmurs before falling asleep.

My mother leans back in her chair and closes her eyes. She probably hasn't slept much, vigilant on my father's behalf whenever he's doing poorly. I give her shoulder a squeeze. She puts her hand on mine and gives me a squeeze back before releasing my hand.

Now is not the time to rebel. I know what I must do—marry the bride they've chosen for me, to bring my father peace. I stand, bow my head to them both, and take my leave.

I pace the long halls of the palace, restless energy driving me. I know my duty, my responsibility, but I cannot reconcile myself to it.

An hour later, I find myself at Polly's room. I try the door and it's unlocked. I step inside to a quiet room. The light is on, but no Polly. The bathroom door is open. She's probably the type to leave it open, having no sense of modesty or propriety. It tickles me because it's so wrong, so the opposite of everything I've known. She's the rebel I could never be.

"Polly?"

I hear a squeak and then she appears from the floor beside her bed, wearing some fantastic workout clothes, a neon blue sports bra and tiny black spandex shorts. "Hi! I was just doing my planks. It clears my head and tones my core."

My gaze drifts to her flat toned belly, and my mouth goes dry. My fingers tingle with the urge to touch her.

"You've got the sexiest bedroom eyes I've ever seen." She closes the distance, hips swaying, mesmerizing me.

I pull her into my arms and kiss her with all the intensity of what I'm feeling. A long while later, I release her, my eyes locked on hers, wishing things could be different, wishing there was another way. "My bride has been chosen for me. Francesca."

She looks away, her voice quiet. "I figured. She's the only one left."

"Besides you."

She backs away. "Now, we both know that's a

nonstarter. I could never be queen of Villroy. I don't fit in here."

"You will be someone else's wife one day. Some lucky man." She'll marry someone from her kingdom probably. Or maybe she'll be stuck in a soulless alliance of kingdoms as I am. This all feels wrong.

I sink heavily to the bed and rest my elbows on my knees. "I cannot let my father down. He's suffering and needs peace of mind." And then I think of what my father truly needs, what we all need, a way forward for Villroy. Fresh blood with fresh ideas, as my mother said. For the first time it occurs to me that Polly's rebellious nature, her free spirit, could actually be an asset. Something to embrace not restrict.

I straighten as this new idea takes hold. "Maybe the fact that you don't fit the mold is a good thing. You could help make some much-needed changes around here."

She stares at me with so much longing in her eyes I feel hopeful. She understands what I'm asking. If she would agree to be my wife, I would fight for that right. But then she looks away, her lips pressed into a flat line.

"Polly." I hate the desperate tone in my voice. I have never sounded desperate in my life. Nothing has ever mattered as much.

She sits next to me and gives my arm a reassuring squeeze. "Francesca is smart. She was the only one who could figure out the economic puzzle clue. I'm sure she can help with whatever you need. She's a good choice." Her voice is strained. She's trying to do the honorable thing and set me on the proper path.

"She's the king and queen's choice. Not mine."

She leans her cheek against my arm, wrapping her arm around mine and entwining our fingers together. "Thanks for your help, Gabriel. I appreciate it, and the funds from today's challenge will be put to good use. I called home, and everything is all set. It might save a life."

I jolt. "Are you in danger too?"

"No, someone close to me. She's not about to die, but she needs my help to live. I can't tell you any more than that."

I pinch the bridge of my nose. "You're a good person. And I'm the worst kind of person because I don't want to give you your freedom." I drop my hand and turn to her. "I want you to stay."

She slowly shakes her head. "I'm not what you need. Deep down you know that; the king and queen know that. Give it some time and you'll forget all about me."

"I won't. Polly, I will be king and I need—"

"Someone else." She lets go of my hand and shifts away. "You will do your duty because you're an honorable man. It's in your DNA."

"You would refuse me?"

She takes a deep shuddering breath and looks at a point over my shoulder. "Yes."

I cup her cheek, turning her to me, and find her eyes shiny with unshed tears. This isn't easy for her either. Real emotion is banked deep in there, whether she'll admit it or not.

I'm not sure who moves first, but we're drawn together. I slowly lower her to the bed, our mouths fused together, her arms wrapping around me. At least we can have this. For just a little longer.

～

Anna

I'm compartmentalizing, which I'm aces at. There's Anna's life back home as a beautician, and then there's Anna's fairy-tale life living it up in a palace, stealing kisses (and getting dirty) with the crown prince. It's Saturday night and my flight is booked for Monday morning. I'm pretending I'm an honored guest of the royal family this weekend. It's the only way I can enjoy my remaining time here without having a breakdown.

I head to the dining room to meet Gabriel and his younger siblings for dinner. I'm sure they've been summoned for their opinion on the potential brides. Francesca will also be there. Knowing the decision has to be her allows me to completely relax about meeting so many royals at once. Everything has been taken care of for Polly, which is a huge relief. The needed funds were transferred to her private foundation. She'll direct the funds as needed for a primo lawyer. At some point I'm sure someone will notice the money has gone to a lawyer in Florida, but she hopes to be on the move again far away from Florida before that happens. I'll miss her, but I feel good about my part in helping her live life on her terms.

Gabriel is waiting for me, standing tall and proud just outside the dining room. This is a man who would never slouch. He's impossibly gorgeous in a crisp white dress shirt, gray dress pants, and black leather shoes. My cheeks flush and all of my nerve endings tingle like I touched a live wire. It's like my body remembers the sensation of his touch, and just seeing him can have an effect on me. I've got it bad. It's horrible.

I work to keep it light. "Hello, handsome. Am I the first one here?"

He smiles at me warmly, and my pulse thrums through my veins. "Emma and Phillip are in there. Still waiting on the others." He leans down to kiss my cheek. "You look beautiful."

I can't help my wide smile. I'm wearing a green sleeveless dress, low cut, belted waist, and it barely covers my ass. I think it looks fab, but it's not royal material. Gabriel appreciates it because he appreciates *me*. Another time, another place, another life, we might have had something. "Thank you."

He escorts me into the room, his hand on my lower back. I stop short and whisper to him, "You shouldn't touch me in public. It's not fair to Francesca." Thankfully, she's not here yet.

"I don't care."

He's playing this wrong. He's going to screw up everything for something that could never work. He doesn't know who I really am. This place prides itself on long family lines dating back to the Vikings. I read up on it in the royal library. The Rourkes have a proud history, a foundation set in stone, literally, with the first round Viking fortress. The remains of the fortress are not far from the palace, a constant reminder of their heritage. And as much as I've always longed for that kind of foundation, I know I don't belong here.

I rush ahead of his hand and smile at his siblings. "Hi, I'm Polly. Nice to meet you."

Phillip—the royal hottie, I recognize him from his many online pictures—stands to greet me. He takes my hand in a warm clasp. He resembles Gabriel with his thick dark brown hair, beautiful blue-green eyes, and square jaw, except there's an open friendliness to his expression. Maybe Gabriel would've been more like Phillip without the pressure of being the heir.

"I saw you when you first arrived," Phillip says. "You

were so entranced by Gabriel you didn't even notice me in the entrance hall."

My eyes widen and I do a quick mental rewind. He's right. I took one step into the palace and latched onto Gabriel in his tux. He was such a gorgeous mesmerizing presence that I was only dimly aware of the other people standing behind him, fading into the background.

My cheeks flush hot and Phillip chuckles. We both turn to Gabriel. His eyes are warm on mine, a smile playing over his lips. I can't help my goofy smile back. He's still mesmerizing.

"I've heard quite a lot about you, Polly," Phillip says.

I reluctantly turn from Gabriel. "All good, I hope!" *Highly doubtful. The queen probably raged about my impropriety.*

Phillip smiles, but doesn't comment. Instead he gestures toward Emma, who's sitting across the table from him. Emma looks like a proper princess—long dark brown hair parted nearly in the middle, big innocent hazel eyes, cute perky nose, full pink lips. Her dress is modest, a pink short-sleeved sheath.

She smiles at me, remaining seated. "Hello, Polly, I'm Emma. We watched some of the competition on video this morning. You're quite the athlete. Are you supremely motivated to win the right to marry stuffy old Gabriel?" She winks at Gabriel.

"The fact that the competition was filmed was supposed to be a secret," Gabriel replies in a mild reprimand to Emma. He must really love his little sister, because he's usually much gruffer with everyone else. Not so much with me anymore. Sex will do that to a man, soften him up. Actually, more like harden him. *Stop thinking about sex with Gabriel!*

Emma slaps a hand over her mouth, her eyes wide. "I'm so sorry."

"No harm done," Gabriel replies. "Polly knows. Just don't mention it once Francesca arrives." He pulls out a chair for me. "Polly."

I take the offered seat, and he sits at the head of the table on my right. Emma is across from me. Phillip switches seats to sit next to me, which draws a frown from Gabriel.

Gabriel turns to me. "Emma has had an arranged marriage since she was sixteen. They'll marry soon after her twenty-fifth birthday, only a few months from now."

"Are you serious?" I can't help my astonishment. I could see it with the heir, but further down the line they're still being forced into arranged marriages?

Gabriel is matter-of-fact. "It's the preferred way. The recent bridal competition has been very much the exception. My siblings are not required to agree to the arrangement. They can ask for a more suitable candidate. Emma agreed without question to the husband chosen for her. She's always been the most proper of princesses." His speech is more proper now. I wonder if it becomes more casual the more comfortable he is. With me, in the dark of the night, he sounds different—warm, casual, dirty. My favorite.

"I do my duty as I should," she returns.

"We're quite alike in that way," Gabriel says, his eyes warm for his sister.

"The only two in our generation," Phillip says. "Everyone else turned an arrangement down. You two really took to the proper protocol, didn't you?" He turns to me. "Emma's not even close in line to the throne. She just loves rules and the sense of carrying on tradition."

Emma levels Phillip with a hard look. "Without rules the world is chaos. Our traditions are what sustain us. Villroy has a revered history, and that continuity won't be lost on my watch."

"Do you agree, Polly?" Phillip asks.

The truth is I can see both sides. There's freedom in making your own decisions, but there's also something beautiful about taking your place in a revered history. That sense of rooted tradition on Villroy must give them a built-in sense of their place in the world. Then I think of Gabriel and shape my answer in a way that will set him on the right path.

"I suppose rules and tradition can be important."

Phillip's eyes dance with good humor. "And are you a rule follower?"

I snort-laugh. "No." *Oops! Too much me.* "I mean, yes. I've been raised to follow the royal protocol of my king-dom." I have to remember to stick to the princess script.

Phillip smiles at me. "But it's not easy, right?"

I laugh. "Right."

"So tell me all about you. Were you raised in the US?"

All eyes are on me. I can't screw this up for Polly this late in the game. The less I say, the better. "Partly."

"And why is that?"

I stick with one-word answers. "Education."

Phillip nods once. "Our sister Silvia studied in the US. You must've been there quite a while to pick up the accent."

"Mmm-hmm." I focus on arranging my napkin in my lap and order my cheeks to stop flushing hot. This is the first time I've had to answer so many direct questions about Polly.

The door to the dining room opens. Saved! The

arrival of not one, not two, but *three* handsome princes is a welcome sight. They're dressed similarly in button-down shirts and tailored pants, all of them with the same thick dark brown hair and tall muscular build. One has a neatly trimmed beard; the other two have sexy scruff.

"There's the royal bachelor, star of the Rourke reality show!" the one with the beard exclaims, pointing at Gabriel. He holds a pretend microphone out to him. "Who will you choose, Polly or Francesca?"

Gabriel glares at him. "Idiot. That was supposed to be a secret. Luckily for you, Polly already knows. Do *not* mention anything about the reality show in front of Francesca. She's due any moment."

Beard man grins down at me, completely unrepentant. His eyes match Gabriel's aquamarine color. "Sorry and hello, Princess Polly. I'm Lucas." He shakes my hand and turns to Gabriel. "We all watched the show earlier when we visited Father. They forgot to have a rose ceremony, though."

"Enough," Gabriel says.

Lucas salutes him and turns to me, hitching a thumb toward his newly arrived brothers. "The ugly one is Oscar; the crafty one is Adrian."

Oscar flashes a smile, and he's stunningly gorgeous. Honestly, if I were picking, I'd say he should be called the royal hottie in the press. Gabriel is obviously the most gorgeous, but he's above all that kind of nonsense.

Oscar takes my hand and kisses the back of it. His aquamarine eyes are warm on mine. "I can only hope one day to transform from ugly duckling into a swan. So nice to meet you, Polly."

I actually blush. "Thank you. You too."

Adrian greets me warmly—hazel eyes on that one—before taking the seat next to Emma.

I turn to Gabriel and whisper, "Why did he call Adrian crafty?"

"He's a card shark."

"Ah."

"Silvia just arrived," Lucas tells Gabriel. "She went straight to Father." That's his youngest sister, Adrian's twin.

Gabriel inclines his head.

"That's everyone, right?" I ask Gabriel. "Where's Francesca?"

"I don't know." Gabriel signals to a servant to check on her.

An uneasy feeling goes through me. What if she bailed? Or fell ill? I don't think I can be the sole focus of five princes and a princess without slipping up somewhere.

Lucas grins at Gabriel, his teeth a flash of white against his dark beard. "I can't believe you of all people went along with this competition. Temporary insanity? It's the only reasonable explanation."

"It was the least I could do for our father given his condition," Gabriel says.

"I thought we weren't to speak of it to outsiders," Emma whispers.

All eyes turn to me. I look to Gabriel.

Gabriel exhales sharply. "I've shared with Polly because she's going through something similar with her father."

His siblings offer quiet sympathy to me. I nod, blinking rapidly as I think of Mike.

Gabriel continues. "This competition has brought him

some happiness in his last days. I'm sorry I shielded you from that truth. He doesn't have much longer."

Suddenly the importance of Gabriel choosing the right bride hits me. I knew his father was in bad shape, but I hadn't realized he was in his last days. No wonder they had this crazy competition, narrowing us down within a week. He must choose Francesca. Bile rises in my throat. I knew he'd marry another, but the reality of it so soon is hard to stomach.

"What?" Lucas exclaims. "I visited with him earlier, and he didn't say a word about it. In fact, he was joking with me."

"He shields you as well," Gabriel says. "He wants you to enjoy your life. I want you to have a chance to say goodbye."

The room goes quiet.

"Is it really his last days?" Phillip asks. "Is that what the doctor said?"

"The doctor says there's nothing more that can be done," Gabriel says bluntly. "He's definitely worse, in more pain, sleeping more, wasting away." His voice catches, and my own throat tightens in sympathy. He clears his throat. "We need to make arrangements for the future of Villroy. We must be prepared."

Another long silence as the painful truth sinks in. I'm glad his siblings know. For too long, Gabriel shouldered the burden alone. Now they can comfort each other.

Lucas gestures over to me. "I suppose you're part of the future arrangements. Gabriel has confided in you. He doesn't confide in anyone." That last part comes out bitter. I can't blame him. It must suck to be left out of something so important.

I shift in my seat, my chest tight because I know I'm

not part of Gabriel's future. "Actually, Francesca is a wonderful candidate. I've told Gabriel he should choose her." My voice cracks, and I cover with a big fat lie. "I wish them both the best." What I really wish is that Gabriel weren't the crown prince tied to duty and obligation. I can't look at him, though I feel his eyes on me.

"It's not up to Gabriel, though, is it?" Emma asks. "As the heir, he needs approval from the king and queen."

"They want Francesca too." I turn to Gabriel. "That's what you said."

Gabriel clenches his jaw.

"Hello?" Lucas looks back and forth between Gabriel and me before asking Gabriel, "If the decision has already been made, then why're we all meeting Polly?" He turns to me. "Not that we don't want to have dinner with you, but I thought I was supposed to report back—"

"Lucas!" Emma exclaims. "Such rudeness. Polly, we're all very glad to meet you regardless of the competition. Perhaps we should start with a round of drinks for everyone." She gestures to a servant.

"Great idea!" I practically shout.

All eyes turn to me.

I circle a finger in the air. "Par-tay."

Gabriel remains stone-cold serious, but his brothers crack up. Emma's lips purse, probably because I'm not acting like a proper princess.

It will be such a relief not to have to fake it anymore. But then that would mean no more Gabriel...I stop myself. No. I'm going to enjoy tonight as a guest of the royal family. Period.

12

Gabriel

By the time we get to dessert, it's clear Phillip adores Polly. In fact, he's become so chummy with her and, yes, flirty, I can barely stomach it. Francesca is here, sitting next to Adrian, but mostly talking to Emma. The two women get along well, both of them raised similarly with a sense of propriety and decorum. I can't believe at one point I actually wanted that in a bride.

Oscar rises from the table. "Anyone want to join me on the roof for drinks?" He's always up for more partying.

I want Polly to myself, but I can't make it obvious with Francesca here. I'm about to claim I'm tired when Polly says, "Sure!"

He smiles, crosses to her, and pulls out her chair, playing the gentleman prince. Another of my brothers I'll have to keep an eye on. They all think I'm meant for Francesca, so Polly is fair game. I'll be damned if I'm sharing her during our last weekend together.

"A girl after my own heart," Oscar says. "You'll love it

up there. It's a private rooftop garden, and the view is spectacular. You can see the whole island."

"I'll join you," Phillip says.

Everyone wants to go except Emma, who returns to her room. She's strict about her bedtime, keeping to the same hours day in, day out. I don't judge. She's the only one of us who's always well rested and bright-eyed in the morning. Silvia remained with our father, alarmed at the change in him since her last visit six months ago. She lives in the US now with her husband and hadn't known how poorly our father was doing.

I stand. "I'll go as well." I turn to Francesca. "Are you coming?"

"Of course," she murmurs, her eyes downcast. "If Your Highness would like me there." She will be an agreeable wife, quiet, modest, refined. Everything that Polly is not.

"It will give us time to get to know each other better." The words taste bitter on my tongue. I wait while she has a quick conversation with her maid, an older woman who I suspect is her chaperone. She's been with her for every occasion. Polly leaves with my brothers, giving me a little wave goodbye.

I incline my head, my jaw tight. All I want is to go back to my room with Polly. I've become a sex fiend because of her. Every joining is hotter than the one before. She holds nothing back, and I'm always greedy for more. Just thinking about it is getting me hot. I force my thoughts to unpleasant things like tedious charity dinners filled with idle small talk. I shudder. I hate small talk.

Finally, Francesca and her maid seem to have reached the decision that they will both be going to the roof. I lead them through the east wing at a brisk pace and climb the stairs to the flat rooftop garden. It can hold fifty people and is strictly for the royal family. Though Phillip did host a bachelor party for the last disastrous wedding that was here. He did a lot of things he shouldn't have in the name of launching Villroy as a destination-wedding locale. I should be thankful it was a train wreck, because even he had to admit it was a bad idea.

The drinks are flowing, the lights built into the stone floor give off a warm glow, and jazz plays softly through nearby speakers. It's a warm June night, stars twinkling in the sky, and the moment feels ripe for romance. *Since when am I a romantic?* Maybe knowing I'll lose my father soon has made me more emotional. Or maybe it's *her*.

My gaze lands on Polly, who's laughing at something Phillip is saying. I find myself smiling just watching her laugh. She's lit up, beautiful in her open enjoyment of life. Slowly, I get the feeling someone is watching me. I turn and meet Francesca's eyes. She's standing a short distance away. I have not been fair to her.

I cross to her. "Would you like to dance?"

She looks uneasy. "No one is dancing, Your Highness." She looks at my toes. "It would not be proper."

"Very well. Can I get you a drink?"

"No, thank you."

I squash my irritation at her prim and proper ways and work for pleasant conversation. "What do you think of the competition?"

She meets my eyes briefly before looking to the side. "It was…difficult, but I know the reward will be worth it." She means me.

"Thank you."

Polly lets out a squeal, and I turn just as Lucas is bending her backward over his arm. Are my brothers passing her around? She was just laughing with Phillip.

Lucas pulls her back upright and they're dancing a fast tango. I can't stop staring. They look good together and they dance in perfect synch. My gut clenches. *Dammit. She is mine.*

Oscar taps him on the shoulder and gestures to be let in. Lucas hands Polly over to Oscar, who pulls her into a slow waltz. She looks over his shoulder to grin at Lucas, who's miming crying tears.

I'm done sharing. I take a step toward Polly when Francesca says, "She cannot win the competition. She's unsuited to be queen."

I know this, but I've heard it one too many times. "That's for me to decide," I snap and stride over to Polly and Oscar without a backward glance.

"My turn," I growl at Oscar.

"No way," Oscar says. "I get at least this song."

I shove him away, and he lets me, holding up his palms. "Okay, big guy," he says with a laugh. "Jealous much?"

I ignore that because I am never jealous. I'm above that pettiness. It was simply my turn. I pull Polly flush against my body, one arm banded around her waist, the other holding her hand as I lead her in a slow sway. The tension that built up all night immediately eases, having her back in my arms.

She puts a hand on my shoulder and goes up on tiptoe to whisper in my ear, "As much as I enjoy dancing with you, Francesca is going to throw me off this roof if you don't back off. She's glaring an army of daggers at me."

"I asked her to dance and she refused. My duty is done."

"She refused? I don't get it. Doesn't she know what a hottie you are?"

I grin, loving her casual slang. "Apparently not. Maybe she only wants me for my kingdom."

"And I thought she was so smart." She looks around. "Oh no! Gabriel, she left. She must've been insulted by watching you dance with me." She gives me a small shove, but I'm not going anywhere. "Go to her and make amends. She should know you care about her."

Except I don't. Not at all. I lower my voice. "You could stay."

She tries to pull away, but I tighten my hold. Her eyes are wide, pleading with me. "I'm sorry, I'm not…I can't." She twists in my arms. "Let's get a drink!"

"After our dance."

She sighs dramatically, but a moment later she's resting her cheek on my chest, right over my heart. She's not indifferent to me. She may even return the depth of feeling coursing through me every time I see her.

I lean down to her ear and whisper, "My parents had an arranged marriage that turned into love. I want that too." I hold my breath. I'm telling her I love her, my heart waving in the wind.

She pulls away, crossing her arms tightly. "Francesca is your arranged marriage that could turn into love if you just gave her a fair chance."

Every part of me reaches out to her—body, heart, and soul. "I want you. Polly, I love you."

She stares at me, frowning, looking like she's trying not to cry.

I step closer, wanting to hold her again, erase the pain from her eyes. "Polly."

"Don't do that," she whispers. "I don't deserve your love."

"What do you mean?"

"Your dance is done already?" Phillip asks, appearing out of nowhere. "My turn." He offers his hand to Polly, and she takes it with a tight smile.

I stalk away and pour myself a whiskey from the liquor cart. It's not that I care that Phillip is slow dancing with Polly. Okay, I do. Too much. It's that she won't even consider love as a factor bigger than all the other trappings that go along with my life. Of course she deserves my love. She's everything I could ever want, everything I need.

Oscar and Lucas join me by the liquor cart. "Hello, prince charming," Lucas drawls.

"Why, hello," Oscar replies.

They laugh. Lucas elbows Oscar. "You know who I mean, Mr. Stick-Up-His-Ass."

My eyes are glued to Polly. "Fuck off," I snarl at my annoying little brothers. When neither of them moves, I glare at them.

They blithely ignore me. Lucas pours himself some scotch. Oscar holds up his glass and Lucas splashes some in for him too. They sip and turn to watch Polly. I do too. She is undeniably sexy dancing under the moonlight, her body sensuous in every movement as Phillip takes her hand and leads her in a slow twirl. Phillip has always had women falling at his feet with his warm easy charm. Too bad he's a monogamist at heart because that didn't work out for him so well. His five-year relationship ended in a spectacularly public way for the former golden couple. He was a wreck, which is probably why he rutted his way through Europe, inciting a firestorm of media attention. He's settling down again; maybe he's ready for another relationship. It will not be with Polly.

"Polly's great," Lucas says.

I stiffen. I'm in no mood for their teasing.

"Oh, yeah. Fantastic," Oscar puts in.

I glare at them. "Stop talking about her."

Lucas stage-whispers to Oscar, "He likes her."

Oscar grins. "Does he *like* her like her?"

"Shut up." I give Oscar's head a shove. Such a smartass.

"Seriously," Lucas says, "anyone can see the lust in your eyes where she's concerned. And I get it, but she is not queen material. She actually has a personality instead of a proper princess mask."

"And her clothes are hot," Oscar says. Lucas agrees.

I ignore them. They're trying to get a rise out of me.

Lucas goes on, waxing philosophic. "Even if you gave her a complete queenly makeover, I'm not so sure she's Gabriel material either."

"Better match for Phillip," Oscar puts in.

Polly and Phillip do look good together, comfortable and natural, even though they just met. They're talking like old friends. *No.* Everything in me rebels at the thought. I've never been such a rebel until I met Polly. Maybe I never needed to rebel before.

I turn to my brothers. "You're both idiots."

Lucas rubs his beard thoughtfully. "I don't know. Phillip is a little too much like Gabriel, and Polly looks young."

Phillip turns Polly in a slow circle, and he's smiling like she's the best thing to happen to him in years.

Lucas goes on. "I'm thinking a better match would be—"

"Me," I grind out. "I don't care what—"

"Your Highness, I would like to dance now."

The hair on the back of my neck stands on end, and I

slowly turn to see Francesca standing there. How much did she overhear? Fuck. I thought she left. She's alone now, no chaperone. She must've only taken a brief break from watching me dance too closely with another woman. Guilt pricks my conscience. I haven't given her a fair chance. My heart is already taken. Who knew it could happen so quickly, so thoroughly? The least I can do is treat Francesca decently. She probably ditched her chaperone just so she could dance with me.

I take her hand, leading her to dance in a quiet corner. She's stiff, her hand cold, her movements precise. She's clearly had dance lessons.

After a few minutes, her hand remains icy cold. The sun has set, though I still find it a comfortably warm temperature. "Are you cold?" I ask. "We could go back inside."

"I am a little chilly, Your Highness."

"I'll escort you back. Just a moment."

I cross to where Phillip and Polly are now standing, talking amiably. I address Phillip, but I'm really telling Polly what I want her to know. "I'm taking Francesca back to her room, and then I'll return."

"Take your time," Phillip says cheerfully.

Polly offers me a small smile before turning away.

I turn to do my duty, my limbs heavy with every step.

Anna

Every little sound makes me turn, hopeful to see Gabriel again, but no. It's been more than an hour and he hasn't returned from walking Francesca back to her room. I tell myself it's for the best. He's acting the way he should, establishing a good relationship with his future bride. I try to enjoy myself with Oscar, Lucas, Phillip, and Adrian. The four of them are a riot. Adrian got us started on poker, and he and I are a team since I suck at it. He taught me a lot. Still the whole time my mind is on Gabriel. I only have two nights left in the palace before I have to say goodbye to him forever. Did he go to Francesca's room to test their marital compatibility? I hate that I have these thoughts. He is not mine to keep.

Finally, I stand from the card table and make an excuse to go. "It's been great, guys. I'm pretty beat, so I'm going to call it a night."

"Aww, it's early," Adrian says, shuffling the cards. "One more round."

"Even with your tutoring, I'm afraid I still suck." I laugh. "Hopefully I'll see you guys tomorrow."

"We'll be here," Adrian says, dealing out the cards. He stills, lifting his head, his voice hoarse and a little bitter. "No one wants to go far now that we know the truth about my father's condition."

He's angry he was left in the dark. They all are, I imagine. "I think Gabriel was trying to protect you in his big-brother way," I offer.

Adrian scowls. "It's not just him. Our parents kept us in the dark too. We're not children."

I don't know what to say. It's just a horrible situation all around. "I'm so sorry."

Lucas looks up at me. "Tell the truth, Polly, do you really want to marry my brother? He's so not your type."

I bristle. "Why do you say that?"

He lifts his brows. "You know what I mean. You're fun, and he's not."

"You shouldn't be so hard on him," I snap. "He's had a

heavy burden on his shoulders his entire life. Don't assume that just because he doesn't complain that means it was easy. He's strong, so strong you'd never know what was going on underneath that stoic expression." The words keep spilling out. "He's everything a king should be. An honorable man. And you think that's not my type? I should be so lucky to have a man like that." *But I can't have him.* My throat chokes and I can't utter another word.

Four sets of eyes study me with open curiosity.

"Are you okay?" Phillip asks.

"Gabriel deserves your respect," I manage before turning on my heel and making my escape.

As soon as I get to the third floor, I know where I'm going. I can't help myself. I need to see him again before I have to let him go forever.

His door is unlocked. I hope it means he's waiting for me. I really hope he's here and not in Francesca's room.

I slowly open it, step inside, and shut the door behind me, locking it. He's in bed reading and sets the book on the nightstand.

"I told myself to stay away," I blurt.

He gets out of bed and faces me. "I told myself the same thing."

I rush to his side and throw myself in his arms, my heart pounding against my rib cage. He holds me close for a moment before guiding me down on the mattress, his expression tender as he brushes my hair back and cups my jaw.

A breathless moment of charged silence passes, our gazes locked.

His lips meet mine, and I'm home.

13

———

Anna

I collapse onto the mattress, breathing hard, after another marathon sex session in the early dawn. I'm a limp noodle, worn out and well satisfied. The mattress creaks as Gabriel gets out of bed and heads for the en suite bathroom. I'm too tired to move. A few moments later, he's back, and then he's lifting me, pulling me to lie on top of him. He settles the covers over us in a warm cocoon. I rest my head over his heart and listen to the steady thump.

He strokes a hand down my back. "What do you do back home in your kingdom?"

I tense. I hate lying to him.

"Polly?"

I lift my head. The early sunrise filters through the curtains, illuminating his handsome face. His eyes are intent on mine, his jaw relaxed, sporting a five-o'clock shadow. I love this scruffier relaxed version of him.

"You must do something," he prompts.

"I have a lot of responsibilities, and I work hard. I want to achieve something lasting."

He smiles. "I love that."

Encouraged, and still being very much myself, I share from the heart. "I don't think working hard means you don't get to have fun. I try to connect with people. It's so important for people to feel recognized. And a little positivity goes a long way." This is the secret to my loyal salon clients, but I keep that to myself. I've been very focused on a specific dollar goal to own my own salon by thirty, but underpinning all that is something more. I care about my clients. I like making them feel good about themselves. And, yes, I'm a born entrepreneur, independent and driven.

He cradles my face with one hand. "You could be a great help to Villroy, to me—"

"Tell me about your wild days before you were all duty and obligation."

"Please consider staying. That's all I ask."

"I'm tied to my responsibilities back home. It's impossible."

"Not impossible."

I know I can't let it go further. He still thinks I'm a princess. If I tell him the truth, he'll hate me. He's in love with a fantasy.

I shift off of him and sit up. "I should go."

His hand clamps on my wrist. "Stay and I will tell you of my wild days."

I give him a small smile, my heart aching. "I knew you had to have some." I lie on my side and prop my head on my elbow to listen. And then I find myself grinning as he shares his pranks on his younger siblings as a boy, his teenaged makeout sessions in the very cave where we made out (classic), and even some bar fights that got him a lot of bad press.

"That's why I kept a low profile for the past several years," he admits. "I kept out of the press, out of the spotlight, even shaved my beard so I'd be less recognizable. I dishonored my title."

"Oh, please, you could never dishonor your title. You are honor." I stroke his arm in a soothing gesture. "Now I know why I didn't recognize you when we first met and I thought you were the butler. You must've been laughing your ass off on the inside!"

He chuckles. "I might've been if I wasn't so pissed off about all that wedding garbage."

"Furry wedding! It's still hysterical."

We laugh. And then he rolls on top of me and kisses me. I close my eyes and let him carry me away from reality once more.

I sneak back to my room Sunday morning a little later than I planned, hoping I get there in advance of my maid. It's not that I care what she thinks about what I do with Gabriel. That's between me and Gabriel. It's just that I don't want to cause problems with Francesca. Leave it to me to fall for a man I can't have. Maybe that's why I opened up to him, because it was safe. He could never be a serious consideration for me. Probably some deep abandonment orphan issues in there, but I feel too good right now to dwell on it. It's astounding the deep happiness of the moment. The memory of our night together will stick with me for a long time.

I step into my room and let out a breath of relief. Still

empty. I yank back the covers so it looks like I was there, and head for the luxury of the shower. I'm worn out from our night. Both of us knowing time was running out, we didn't want to waste a single moment. I close my eyes in the steamy spray, my mind drifting to all the ways we pleasured each other. I sigh and replay it moment by moment.

As far as I know, there are no more competitions, so after my shower I dress in a cute green and white striped sundress with my sandals. Maybe I can relax on the beach today. Maybe Gabriel and his brothers can join me. It's not the same as just the two of us, but…it's what I can reasonably do given the Francesca situation.

Someone knocks quietly on the door just as I finish getting dressed. Probably Anna. She's a quiet sort.

"Come in!" I call.

Anna steps in, does a completely unnecessary curtsy, and says, "The queen has asked for you to appear in her private sitting room as soon as possible."

Excitement courses through me. The last time I was summoned to the queen's private sitting room, it was to meet Gabriel. "I'll go now."

She follows. "It really is the queen this time."

"What's up?"

"I don't know. She asked for Francesca too."

A vague memory tickles my brain. Gabriel had mentioned that on Sunday we'd meet with the queen. It had completely slipped my mind in my angst over him. "I guess she's going to make her choice today."

"I hope it's you, Your Highness," she says warmly, surprising me.

"Thanks, Anna, I appreciate that. I'm sure you must've noticed I don't fit in so well in the royal mold they have going on here. Things are much looser at home."

"We need more loosening up here. I think you're perfect, ma'am."

I stop short, my throat tight. *Me? Perfect?* I throw my arms around her in a big hug. "You're the best."

She blushes and bobs her head. What a sweetheart.

We arrive in the sitting room, which is not the room I met Gabriel in before. Anna does a quick curtsy and disappears.

The queen sits in a highback chair, dressed impeccably in a lavender short-sleeved dress with a white cardigan, probably cashmere. Her expression is as serious as a heart attack. Gabriel sits adjacent to her on a blue velvet sofa. He smiles at me, but it doesn't reach his eyes. Whatever is about to happen, it can't be good.

I approach the pair and bow my head first to the queen. I curtsy too, though it's tough with the tight fit of my dress. "Good morning, Your Majesty."

"Good morning," she says flatly.

I turn to Gabriel. Our eyes lock in an intense gaze. My pulse skitters, my mouth goes dry, and every nerve ending tingles with electric awareness, tuned in to him. I manage a small curtsy. "Good morning, Your Highness."

"Good morning, Polly." Only it sounds like *I love you.* The warmth in his voice washes over me like a hug. My heart pounds in my ears, and my knees go weak.

The queen arches a brow at him. Apparently she noticed his tone held something more.

Gabriel indicates the matching blue sofa across from him, and I take a seat.

Francesca walks in with her maid, walking at a sedate pace, her eyes downcast. She's dressed in a white lace dress that makes her olive-toned skin glow. It's modest with a high neck and short sleeves, ending past her knees. I can't help but wonder if she was going for a bridal look.

Francesca bows her head to the queen and makes a deep curtsy that she holds for a good five seconds. My curtsy must've been an insult. Finally she lifts her head. "It's an honor to see you again, Your Majesty."

"Thank you. It's a pleasure to see you too, Francesca."

Francesca smiles before turning to Gabriel. Her smile drops as she does another deep curtsy to him. "Your Highness."

"Please have a seat with Polly," Gabriel says.

She shoots me an icy look before sitting at the far end of the sofa away from me. Her maid hovers behind us.

"I'd like some privacy," the queen announces, calling off the staff in the room. A few security guards and the servants who previously helped with the competition immediately exit. "You too," she snaps at Francesca's maid.

The maid sends Francesca a meaningful look, almost like a mother saying *behave*, before curtsying to the queen and Gabriel and walking out the door.

The queen folds her hands in her lap and offers us princesses a small smile. "I've asked you both here this morning for a final interview. Your answer will lead to one of you being named as the future bride of the crown prince, so please think carefully before responding. First, some background. Villroy is in need of a boost to our economy. We've depended on fishing for centuries. It's an integral part of our traditional way of life. Unfortunately, the fish population is declining, which means the fishermen must travel farther out to sea in deeper waters. It's more work and they're bringing less back."

Gabriel speaks up. "We're losing the younger generation in search of better jobs. We need better opportunities for them here. A kingdom made up only of the older generation will quickly die out."

The queen sucks in air through her teeth. I think of her dying husband and understand better why she has seemed so strained every time I've seen her. Of course, that might partly be her reaction to me personally. I seem to rub her the wrong way.

Francesca and I wait quietly for the question. She's on the edge of her seat. I'm not. I won't give it any thought. I'm just going to say the first thing that comes to mind. If for some insane reason, the queen actually chooses me, which I doubt, I'll bow out. But I'd never be so disrespectful as to walk out without answering a question that is so important to the queen personally.

Finally, the queen says, "If you were the future queen, what would you do, along with your husband, to ensure the vitality of Villroy's economy?"

I jump right in, speaking off the top of my head. "Ooh, I know! It's what every commoner would love—live like royalty for a week at the palace. Make it a girls' trip or a honeymoon destination. A one-week stay for an exorbitantly high price. It wouldn't be like the crowd of a wedding party, just a small select group." That actually sounds right up my alley, so I can't help but add, "And give them the full beauty experience too, hair, makeup, nails, facials. Almost like a spa. Well, one thing at a time. Probably just start with one beautician who can do all that." I realize suddenly I'm describing myself and I'm actually jazzed about the idea. "And special beauty products they can purchase to bring home with them, featuring something native to Villroy. Yes! You could also build a day spa with a locally sourced beauty line, set near the beach, but away from the palace." I know Gabriel doesn't want tons of tourists trampling through the palace.

Both the queen and Gabriel are staring at me, their expressions giving nothing away. I'm not sure if they think it's the stupidest idea they've ever heard or I just surprised them. I should shut up now, but my mind is racing with ideas. "I've heard fish oil can do wonders both inside and out."

A long silence follows.

Francesca turns to me. "Are you done?"

"Yes."

She turns to address the queen. "Your Majesty—"

"Seaweed is another possibility," I blurt. "Natural sea salt scrubs." I've got beautician's Tourette's, if that's a thing. I can't seem to stop. "Algae."

Francesca glares at me.

"And now I'm done." I clamp my mouth shut, even though I just had another great idea for the day spa beauty product line—sponges from the sea. Every product would be all-natural and locally sourced. The fishermen could still be involved, but on a different product.

Francesca turns back to the queen. "Your Majesty, I know Villroy has a long proud history. I would want to preserve that traditional way of life. My idea is to fund a new powerful fleet of fishing vessels that would allow the fishermen to take in more haul in waters that weren't reachable to them before. I would be happy to contribute to this fleet personally." She glances at Gabriel, who nods once, before lowering her gaze to the floor.

She's everything I'm not—wealthy, traditional, demure up the wazoo. This was never a competition. She was born for this role. I was born with nothing. I came from nothing, but I will make something of myself. I *have* made something of myself. I've worked hard every day of my life to get where I am today, but no amount of work can ever make me something I'm not.

I stand, drawing everyone's attention. "It's clear to me that Francesca is the better choice in every way. I'm removing myself from the running."

Francesca allows herself a small smile as she looks straight ahead.

The queen says, "Very well. Francesca is the winner. And, Polly, if you hadn't been so quick to declare yourself out of the running, I was about to choose her anyway. I far prefer to preserve our way of life than to have random rowdy people parading through our home."

I bow my head. "Thank you for having me in your lovely home. Goodbye."

"Wait!" Gabriel is on his feet. "Polly, don't go."

"Gabriel," I beg. He's going to make this difficult. I can see it in his wild-eyed look.

"Polly's idea could work," he tells his mother. "And a one-week stay wouldn't be any more inconvenient than this week's competition. Here and gone before you know it. It's like Phillip's idea but better, smaller scale and more controlled. And the day spa is brilliant! So much opportunity for growth there, and it could incorporate the fishing industry through the beauty product line. It has real merit. And it's not like we'd become a resort destination. The spa could attract day-trippers from the mainland." He turns to me, his eyes full of love. "You're brilliant."

My eyes get hot. "Oh, Gabriel, you're brilliant too. I so admire you and all you do." My voice is rough, knowing I need to let him go.

"I choose Polly," he declares.

My lungs seize. *Don't do this.*

"Gabriel!" the queen exclaims, standing in her agitation. "We talked about the proper choice."

"What?" he asks. "That this was all a sham? That you wanted Francesca all along? Well, you don't get to play your little games anymore. I'm done being bandied about as a prize. I love Polly. I choose love, and you of all people should understand loving the person you spend your life with."

The queen is unmoved, her tone steel. "You will learn to love Francesca."

"I won't," he says. "Because my heart is already taken."

It's so romantic I want to swoon. But one look at Francesca sitting stiffly while the two royals argue over her place makes me realize what I need to do. The honorable thing. The only way out.

"My name isn't Polly Lyon," I announce. My legs go wobbly and I sink back to the sofa. Gabriel will never forgive the lie, and I know I've lost him forever. I can't look at him. I stare at my hands and try to gather the strength to walk out the door.

"Who are you?" the queen demands.

I turn to her. "My name is Anna Hebert. I pretended to be Polly, and I'm very sorry." I risk a look at Gabriel, and his face is twisted in fury. "I tried to be as much myself as I could with you, Gabriel. That part was real."

His lip curls and he turns his head away like he can't bear looking at me.

I clear my throat, blinking rapidly. "So it's clear Francesca is the right choice."

Security enters the room, rushing toward me.

"I pressed the alert button," the queen says. "You're a

danger to us, and you must be detained until your departure."

I gulp, my fingers gripping the sofa cushion. "Detained?"

Two guards haul me to my feet, and then my hands are cuffed behind my back.

Panic shoots through me, my fight-or-flight kicking in hard. "Hey! I'm an American! I have rights."

"The dungeon," the queen commands.

"Dungeon!" I shriek. "With spiders?"

Gabriel grimaces.

Francesca remains the picture of decorum, her gaze downcast. Bitch.

The queen says nothing, her expression pure contempt.

I kick and scream, but the four guards easily overpower me. They drag me out of the room, through an endless maze of hallways, down a long flight of stairs to an underground space that's dark and damp. It smells like swamp. There really are jail cells. The air is deathly cold, and I swear I can hear the cries of tortured spirits left to die down here.

"Don't you have a police station?" I ask desperately. "A real prison? Take me there."

"The queen wants this kept quiet," a guard says.

And the queen has absolute power here. My heart races as they drag me along to the farthest cell in the darkest corner. There are thick cobwebs in the corners of this place. Spiders. Probably rats too and whatever crept in from the underneath. I'm shaking from cold and fear, my teeth chattering uncontrollably.

"Please don't put me in there," I cry as one of the guards takes my handcuffs off.

They put me in there. The door clangs shut and he locks it from the outside.

I cross my arms, hugging myself in my thin sundress. The men leave me to my solitary confinement. The only light is through high narrow windows, too narrow for a person to fit through, and there're bars across them anyway. By sundown, it'll be pitch black in here. The spiders and God knows what else will slither across the floor and down the walls undetected, making their way to live prey. Me.

A hysterical laugh bubbles up. I'm living the nightmare I feared for Polly, trapped in a cage. Two princesses walk into a prison cell...I got nothing. The joke falls flat. It's just sad.

There's no one working from the outside for my freedom. The one person who could has turned against me. And who could blame him? I've betrayed his trust.

I sink to the ground in the center of the space, bend my legs, and rest my head on top. Something brushes my arm and I scream, leaping to my feet and slapping at the creepy spider I'm sure touched me.

I will stand all day and all night. I'll be like a horse and sleep standing up, eyes open. I cross my arms, vigilant for whatever might come at me. And then I burst into tears. I've lost Gabriel and there will never be another like him. Not for me.

I gave him his freedom, gave him what he needed to live his life. I don't get to have needs.

I am Anna Hebert, and I am a liar.

14

———

Anna

Imposter princess incarcerated!

Orphan tries to claim the throne!

Beautician turns ugly in war of royal love!

I'm not sure how long I've been standing here in the middle of a spider-infested dungeon, creating awful headlines for myself, but I can't feel my feet anymore. My sundress and sandals are no match for the chilly dungeon. The sun is nearly set, only a dim creeping light slanting through the bars of the window. I'm alert to every noise, every soft swish and scratching of dungeon wildlife.

I deserve to be devoured by rats. I've hurt the man I love, the man who loved me back, who treated me like a jewel. My eyes sting; my cheeks flush with shame. I've embarrassed him while he defended me as his choice in front of the queen and Francesca. And now I've lost him. My lower lip trembles, and I bite down on it hard.

Heavy footsteps descend the stairs. One man. Maybe a guard has returned to bring me some gruel. I'll send him away.

But I might need my strength to fight off the giant rats waiting to gnaw my limbs off.

Do the guards know I have a ten a.m. flight out of Paris tomorrow?

The footsteps slow and a familiar deep voice calls out, extra heavy on the sarcasm, "I'm Polly Lyon and that's no lie."

I wince at my own words to Gabriel the first day we met. "I felt so guilty I just blurted that out."

He appears in front of my cell and glares at me. His blue eyes are cold in the dim light, and it's a wee bit intimidating. "You had us all fooled."

"I can explain."

His lip curls. "Go right ahead. I'm sure it'll be as entertaining as all of your other lies."

I reach through the bars and grab his hand. "This is the truth. You and I were never a lie."

He yanks his hand from mine, and I die a little inside. I soldier on because I need him to know why I did what I did. Maybe one day he'll forgive me, or at least not hate me.

I take a deep breath and then I tell him everything—from meeting my neighbor princess in hiding to her arrest for identity theft and her upcoming court date. I want to lay all the blame at her feet, but I know I was a willing accomplice. "She asked me to come here and collect her inheritance in hopes of hiring a fancy lawyer to quietly help her avoid jail. I didn't know marriage to you was on the table, and I definitely didn't know there were going to be these insane competitions. And, Gabriel, you were sending me these desperate looks, like save me—"

"I was not."

Men never want to ask for help. Doesn't mean they don't need it.

I lift a palm. "And we connected in the garden and after..." My breath hitches. "I take full responsibility for my part in this. I thought I'd be Polly's knight-ess in shining armor."

He hangs his head, shaking it.

I take a deep breath, hoping for forgiveness yet knowing I don't deserve it. "Gabriel, I'm so sorry for hurting you. I wanted to tell you the truth so many times, but I feared exposing Polly, and once we connected, I was afraid to lose you. I know it's dumb that I hung on to you knowing I had to let you go, but I've never felt this way before." My voice chokes. "I just wanted to be close to you for as long as I could. I love you."

He stares at me, his expression hard. He hates me.

My eyes well. "I wish I could be the princess you need. I'm so very sorry for betraying your trust. I just want you to know I was as much myself with you as I could be. You made me feel so special. No one has ever made me feel the way you did."

He looks at me for a long tense moment. "Everything makes so much sense now, all of the ways that you didn't fit the mold. In fact, I can't believe I didn't see through your flimsy attempts at playing princess. You are the most brash, ill-mannered person I've ever met."

"But you love me anyway?" I bat my lashes at him, trying for a joking tone, but some part of me desperately hopes that he does. He said he loved me before, and this morning he chose me for a bride when Francesca would've been the easy choice.

He glowers down at me for a moment before his gaze drops to my cleavage and continues all the way down to my scarlet red toenails peeking out of my sandals. He jerks his head up to meet my eyes. "And you dress too sexy for a proper princess."

"And that does it for you." It's not a question. We both know he's hot for me, and I've been a goner since the Gabriel-fresh-from-the-shower show.

"Your accent," he mutters, looking at the ceiling. "I thought it was from your education in the US."

"Maybe you believed in my lie because you needed someone different around here to shake up the status quo. I never had any bad intentions, I swear. I never expected to fall for you so fast, so deep. It's crazy how much I love you." *And hopeless.*

He remains stone-cold silent, his expression closed against me.

An icy shiver runs through me, and my teeth chatter. "Maybe one day you can f-forgive me." I cross my arms, hugging myself. "I'll never forget our t-time together."

He exhales sharply. "I'm getting you out of here."

"Thank you!" I call to his retreating back.

Several excruciating minutes later, where I fear he's changed his mind and decided to leave me to the spiders and giant rats, he returns with the key and springs me free.

I leap into his arms, wrapping my arms and legs around him and peppering his face with kisses. "Thank you, thank you, thank you."

"You should never have been thrown in the dungeon in the first place," he mutters, walking with me in his arms toward the stairs.

"The queen hates me."

"More of a strong dislike. She's not in a good place."

I squeeze him tight. "You saved me from the spiders

and giant rats."

"I suppose I'm your knight in shining armor."

"You definitely are."

He sets me down at the top of the stairs. "What am I going to do with you, Polly?"

"It's Anna."

He closes his eyes for a second. "Yes, Anna." His eyes meet mine in a rueful look. "Polly suited you."

"It is a cute nickname." I go up on tiptoe and whisper, "Take me to your room for one last night together. I leave in the morning."

He grabs my hand and walks at a brisk pace, taking me in a convoluted path, through a large kitchen, up a back staircase, and through a series of hallways I've never seen before. Finally, we arrive in the upstairs hallway that leads to his room. He's hiding me. From the queen or from Francesca, I don't know and I don't care. All that matters is that I get to have him one last time.

We arrive in his room and he shuts the door and locks it. I whip off my sundress, standing in only my thong and heels. I skipped the bra since it was a skinny-strapped halter top. I'm wearing little flower pasties for modesty's sake. See? I can do modesty.

He slaps a hand over his forehead. "You weren't a virgin either, were you?"

"Welp, the real Polly is a virgin." I peel off the pasties and flick them over my shoulder. "And I wanted you so badly. Would you rather we never touched each other?"

He's on me in a flash, pulling me roughly to him. His rock-hard erection presses insistently into my stomach. "You have no idea how difficult it was for me to go slow. I was so careful I sweated through that first time. I've never been with a virgin before."

I slide my fingers through his hair, cupping the back of his warm neck. "You were wonderful. I think that's when I fell in love with you."

He freezes in place. *Rewind. Stop loving on him!* He's changed his mind on the whole love thing because I'm a liar who betrayed him. My gut rolls, and I think longingly of the dungeon with its welcoming cobweb decor.

I pull away, but he holds tight and draws me closer, turning me in his arms, his chest warming my bare back. He places a soft kiss on the side of my neck, and I melt against him, closing my eyes.

"Who are you, Anna? What parts of you were real?"

I open my eyes and see our reflection in a full-length freestanding antique mirror. He's still dressed. I'm in a thong and high-heeled sandals, but I'm not cold with his arms wrapped around me. Our eyes meet in the mirror. I so want to reach him, to feel close to him again. "My heart, my personality, my age, my dying father—all very real. Though technically he's my foster father. Mike. I'm an orphan. Well, I recently learned I'm what you'd call a 'foundling,' which means my parents are alive and gave me up for adoption. I was never adopted, so orphan fits the way I've always felt. Anyway, I bounced through a lot of foster homes. They're, like, temporary homes for kids with no family. I mean, kids don't always bounce as much as I do. I got in a lot of fights with the other girls because I wouldn't put up with their bullshit and got kicked out."

"Now I see why you were such a good competitor. You play to win."

I laugh a little. "I guess it's in my nature. Mike was my last foster home when I was seventeen. He's the closest thing to a dad I ever had." My voice comes out hoarse, my throat tight. I clear my throat. "He was a handyman. He could fix literally anything—electric, plumbing, drywall, appliances, you name it. He taught me. It's not hard once you have the knowledge and the right tools. I can fix most anything now too." *Almost anything. I can't fix us.*

His brows lift in surprise. "Can you?"

"Yes," I say softly. "I'm the super at my apartment building and do repairs for the tenants. My idea for a ladies' week spa-like experience at the palace was based on my own expertise. I was imagining fixing up a suite to make the royal fantasy come true. I'm also a beautician at a high-end salon. I'm in demand as a hairdresser, but I can do nails and facials. I stay current on all the latest beauty treatments. My dream is to own my own salon by thirty, so I've been socking money away whenever I can. I work hard, like I told you before, and I'm very driven."

He turns me to face him and draws me close, hugging me. I hug him back. It feels good, like he's letting me in a little. I can't ask for more than that.

His voice rumbles near my ear. "Your last name is Hebert. Is that French?"

I look up at him. "Yeah, my father was part French, from Louisiana. When I turned eighteen, I did some research trying to find my biological parents. My mother was from Florida and only fifteen when she had me. Anyway, she wasn't interested in a reunion, but she did tell me a little about my dad. She gave me his last name, hoping someone in his family would take me in. They were well off. No dice. I never tried to find him since she said he hadn't wanted me."

He cradles my jaw with one big hand, his eyes meeting mine. "I'm sorry."

My throat tightens. "It's okay. I've been on my own for a long time."

He smooths my hair back from my face. "You won't be anymore."

Hot tears sting my eyes. "Gabriel, please, don't do anything crazy on account of me—"

His mouth crashes down over mine. All thoughts fly from my mind. Suddenly we're grabbing each other, devouring each other, wild and hungry. His hand delves between my legs, and he groans right along with my moan.

"So wet," he rasps.

"Yes," I manage on a sharp exhale as his fingers toy with me. He plays my body expertly now. Within minutes my hips are lifting, seeking more of his touch, my breath harsh, out of my mind with need.

He releases me suddenly. "Go to the bed and lie on your stomach."

I pull my thong off and slip off my sandals. His eyes are hot on mine, his fingers rapidly undoing the buttons of his shirt. I reach out to help him with the button on his pants, and he slowly shakes his head.

"Bed now," he growls.

A shiver of excitement runs through me. Gloves are off now that he knows he's not dealing with a virgin princess. Before he was holding back on me, restraining himself, though I saw glimpses of the true Gabriel.

I do as he says, lying on the bed on my stomach. I peek over my shoulder at him. "What's taking so long?"

"Pol—Anna. Fuck."

"Yes."

He gives my ass a light slap and lifts my hips. "You have no idea how much I wanted you just like this."

I get my elbows under me and go on all fours. "Then take me."

He cups my ass with both hands, and I spread my legs wider in invitation. He trails his fingers straight up my spine, squeezes the nape of my neck, and presses my head down into the pillow. I'm hot and wet and so ready. Gabriel has brought me the most intense pleasure of my life, and I want to give him what he needs.

I hear the nightstand drawer, the rustle of a condom, and then he's back, his fingers gripping my hips tightly as he takes me in one deep thrust. I gasp at the sudden filling of my body.

He grunts, and then he's pounding into me, pulling my hips back for each deep thrust. This version of Gabriel takes and takes and takes. It's wild, animal, primal. I give myself over to it. I love it, and I love him. He's showing me who he is on the most basic level. He fills me up, pushing me closer and closer to the edge.

I'm panting, fever hot, possessed by him. His hand snakes around, sliding to pleasure central, stroking me rapidly. *Yes!* I'm so freaking close. He knows it, can feel me tightening around him, and he plays that line expertly. Fast and hard; slow and deep. I'm trembling under him. Every nerve ending is on fire.

"Gabriel," I gasp out. "Please. I'm so close. Please, please, please."

He covers me, leaning forward to rasp into my ear, "Not yet, my nonvirgin nonprincess."

I groan long and loud.

He chuckles and then he gets back to the business of making me insane. We are rutting beasts, drenched in sweat, slapping together with animal grunts and groans. I'm breathless as he pumps into me, his fingers alternating stroking, circling, tapping. The man is wicked. I'm between begging and screaming *payback* when he gentles.

I pant, waiting for whatever comes next.

His teeth tug my earlobe. "Would you like me to give you your release?"

"Yes."

"You don't sound desperate enough." He thrusts deep and stills.

I push back into him, eager for more. "I'm so desperate."

He strokes me lazily, like he's not burning hot, his skin singeing my back.

I lift my head and look at him over my shoulder. "Fuck me, Gabriel. Fuck me hard and deep. I want to feel you lose control."

He grips my hair and kisses me hard. "I fucking love you."

My lips part in surprise, the emotion in his voice real and raw.

And then he's pushing my head back down, taking me the way we both need. My mind clouds, every hard thrust, every demanding stroke of his fingers burning through me. It's love, it's a claiming, and I want it as much as he does. I break on a harsh cry, shuddering around him, the pleasure bursting through me. He's got me tight, rocking into me, carrying me further, deeper, the pleasure never ending.

His teeth clamp on the crook of my neck, sending another shock through me as he lets go, rocking me with the force of it. He holds me for a long moment, tight against him, before slowly withdrawing and rolling onto the bed next to me.

I collapse to the mattress.

"This ass," he says, giving me a light slap and then a caress. "Perfection."

I turn my head to face him. "That's the first time I've heard that one. Perfect ass? High praise."

He flashes a wide smile before pulling me into his arms, chest to chest, his leg thrusting between mine. A moan escapes; I'm still so sensitive. He cups my jaw, lifting my face to his, and kisses me tenderly. *He loves me.* I can feel it deep inside, in the way he touches me, whether he's being his most aggressive self or his most tender self. He's giving me all of him.

I can never be accepted here as his wife. I have only this moment, so I snuggle closer and hold him tight to me.

He wakes me twice more in the night, giving me all of him, and I do the same, holding nothing back. The passion rages between us, a last fiery goodbye.

I wake at dawn and quickly get ready, letting him sleep. Once I'm freshly showered and dressed, I stand next to the bed and admire him for a long moment. He's on his side facing me, with his arm and leg still stretched out where I would've been. His thick brown hair is tousled from my fingers, his lashes fanning his cheeks, giving him a softer look, his square jaw sporting morning stubble. I resist the urge to trace the line of his jaw. Distance is the only thing that will make leaving him easier. He's just too tempting.

"Gabriel, wake up." I give his shoulder a nudge. "I have to go. I have to catch the ferry to the—ah!"

He's yanked me right on top of him, rolling to his back. "Mmm," he says, running his hands down my back and cupping my ass. "This is nice."

Hot tears burn my eyes. I lift my head, and he gazes back at me steadily. Knowing I'll never see him again, I spill my guts. "I just want you to know I'll never forget my time here with you. You are *magnificent*, the best, most gorgeous, sexiest, most honorable man I've ever met. And smart and strong and tender in all the right ways, and I love you. I've never felt like this before, the depth of my feelings shocks me, and I know the timing is bad, and my background isn't what you need. Not to mention the queen hates—" he opens his mouth to protest that, and I amend to a gentler term "—I mean, greatly dislikes me, probably the king too. No one would accept me as your bride, and it's only because I love you so much that I'm willing to let you go."

His arms tighten around me in a crushing hug.

"I can't breathe," I manage.

He loosens his hold. "So you're letting me go to do the honorable thing."

"Yes. And I know you would do the same in my shoes. You've been raised to do your duty."

He rolls me under him and kisses me, biting my lower lip hard enough to sting. I indulge myself in one last decadent kiss, my legs spreading to cradle him close.

He groans into my mouth and breaks the kiss. "Stay here."

"I'm going to miss my flight."

"I'll put you on the private jet."

"Oh."

He holds my chin and looks deep into my eyes. "If you leave this bed, I will hunt you down and tie you to the bedposts. You'll be at my mercy, and I will not be gentle."

I smile cheekily. "Now you're making me want to leave the bed. Bondage with you? Hell yeah."

He flashes a smile before getting serious again. "Don't move," he orders, getting off me and out of bed. "I have to go talk to my brother."

"Which one? Why?"

He keeps walking, grabbing clothes from the dresser and yanking them on. The flex of muscle momentarily distracts me as he pulls on a shirt, boxer briefs, and pants. He shoves his feet into loafers and heads for the door.

"Gabriel? Are you going to tell him how I'm a big liar and the worst kind of nonvirgin nonprincess person there is?"

"Yes."

I throw a pillow at him. "For real. Don't do anything crazy. You belong on that throne. Everyone knows it. And we all know I'm not fit to be queen. I'm not proper enough and my bloodlines are muddied."

"No argument there," he throws over his shoulder and leaves.

I flop back on the mattress. He's bought us a little time with the private jet, and I know I'm the worst kind of selfish person because all I can think about is him returning to bed and taking me in his rough tender way. My throat gets tight, eyes hot. *Don't cry! You can cry all you want on the flight home.* I should leave right this moment, rip him off like a Band-Aid, but instead I lie here and relive moment by moment every wonderful time I've had with him.

I'm going to be wrecked without him.

But staying means I'll be wrecking him, his life, his destiny as king. And I can't let that happen. Gabriel Rourke was born to be king.

With my last ounce of willpower, I get out of bed and race back to my room to pack. I need to hurry to catch my flight. I can't let Gabriel jeopardize his birthright, and I fear that's what he's about to do.

This is the right thing for both of us. One day he'll understand and forgive me.

15

———

Gabriel

I'm dying to get back to Polly. Anna. Pollyanna. Ha. She is a cheerful vivacious woman, such a contrast to my more serious self. I want that in my life; I want her. I'm nearly delirious from lack of sleep and the sudden turn of events, but there's one more thing I have to do. I knock on the door of my parents' suite.

The maid who lets me in is smiling. She does a quick bobbing curtsy. "The king is awake and doing better today."

"That's great news, thank you." My task will be so much easier now.

I go to my father's bedside. He's propped up on pillows, holding my mother's hand in her usual bedside chair. They're talking quietly to each other, so engrossed in conversation they don't notice me right away.

I clear my throat. "I heard you're feeling better."

My father gives me a weak smile. "The pain is manageable. There is no *better*, I'm afraid."

My mother is solemn. "Where have you been?

Francesca told me she hasn't seen you since she was declared your intended yesterday morning."

I take a deep breath. "I love Anna. I will marry her or abdicate the throne."

"No!" my mother shouts. She takes a deep breath, regaining her composure, her voice shaking with rage. "You will do no such thing."

My father raises a hand, signaling for her to wait. "Gabriel, *you* are the leadership Villroy needs. We've put a lot of time and energy into preparing you for this role. None of your siblings have had the same. They're untested and unready."

"I've spoken to Phillip. He says he'll do it. He wants me to be happy."

"No," my mother says firmly.

My happiness has never factored with them.

My father scowls. "This is just like with Daniel. Selfish. He fell in love with a commoner, abdicated, and then I had to step into a role I never wanted. It was forced on me." He's speaking about my uncle, who, ironically, also fell in love with an American. I can see why he thinks it's the same thing with me, but it's not.

I make my case as calmly as possible. "Phillip says if I guide him in the beginning, he's willing. It's not being forced upon him." He surprised me with his gracious acceptance. Maybe because he knew about the dire circumstances of our father's illness and the urgent need to find a way forward for Villroy. He was the only one I confided the seriousness of the situation to because he's next in line for the throne. It occurs to me I did my younger siblings a disservice by not sharing the full picture. The Rourke legacy isn't just for the king, it's for the entire family, and that means it's time to stop shielding my younger brothers and sisters from reality and get them involved. Villroy is one generation away from collapse. One thing at a time. First I must secure a future for me and Anna.

"You cannot live here with that lying imposter," my mother declares. "You will be exiled just as your uncle was."

Acid churns in my stomach at the harsh cruelty. Never see my family again? Villroy is a living, breathing part of me. I don't know who I am without the island and my family. I am nothing.

My father's head swivels toward hers. They exchange a silent communication before he turns back to me. I hope that means she's bluffing about exiling me.

"Have you really thought about this?" my father asks. "You've only known the woman for a little over a week."

"It's an infatuation," my mother says. "You want to sow your last oat before marriage."

I shove a hand in my hair. "It's not like that. I'm thirty years old. I know what I want."

"She lies," my mother hisses. "She's misled you with false feelings."

"She only lied to help Polly. The real Polly was practically under lock and key at home and escaped to the US. She's now in Florida, about to go to trial for identity theft."

My mother jumps. "My God, we have to get in touch with her people." My father agrees.

"No. That's the whole reason Anna pretended to be her. She was supposed to collect Polly's inheritance—that false claim you dangled to lure women here—and use the money to get her a good lawyer to keep it quiet. The real Polly feared a conviction would expose her true identity.

Her family would disown her and she'd be a target in prison."

"Why would she want to escape Beaumont?" my father asks. "She was a princess living in paradise."

"She was being pressured to marry a dishonorable man." Anna explained it to me last night. I think of the real Polly, a virgin princess in an old-school monarchy, being pressured to marry a sleazy businessman. Damn, I knowingly defiled a virgin princess. And here Anna's been singing my praises as an honorable man. Of course, now I know Anna wasn't a virgin. Even so, my honor has a serious dent in it.

My mother's voice rises. "Our sources said she is an eligible single royal."

"She still is. She left before things progressed further with this other man." I take them both in, pleading with them to understand how we got to this point. "Anna says she's sent Polly the funds she needs for a lawyer through Polly's private foundation from her prize winnings. Do you understand the kind of person she is? She acted honorably, selflessly." These are the traits of a queen, but I keep that to myself. I don't need Anna to be queen. I just need her by my side.

My mother frowns. "I still say we should contact her people. A princess facing jail, all alone—"

"Stay out of it," I bark. "Let her live her life on her terms." My tone is harsh because I'm also talking about myself.

My mother's eyes narrow because she knows it too.

I lift my palms. "Please. All I'm asking is for you to give Anna a chance. I choose her, and she wants me to choose the crown."

"Bring her here," my father says. "Right away. I want

to hear from her directly what she thinks about ruining your life."

"It's not ruining it!"

My father turns to my mother. Neither of them speak. I've been dismissed.

I need to bring Anna to meet my father. It's the only chance we have. My mother is already closed against her.

I bow my head and quickly take my leave. I have an inkling of hope now. I go straight to my room, open the door, and stride inside. "Anna, my father wants…Anna?" She's not in bed. I quickly check the en suite bathroom. I wasn't gone that long.

Dammit! I told her to stay put. I couldn't tell her what I was planning because I didn't know if it would go in my favor.

I grab the phone and call the servants' quarters, looking for Anna's maid, who I just now realize is also named Anna. Weird coincidence.

"She's gone, Your Highness," her maid says. "She left on the ferry."

"When?"

"Maybe fifteen minutes ago."

I hang up. The ferry is no match for the sleek speed of our yacht.

Anna

The other ferry passengers give me a wide berth as I sit on a bench bawling my eyes out with big gulping sobs. Even wearing my favorite leopard-print dress and heels can't give me the strength to face this goodbye. Villroy fades in the distance, a blurry view through my tears, almost like a mirage I imagined. Except this pain is too real. Everything hurts—my eyes, my throat, my heart.

Eventually I run out of tears, lean on the deck rail, and rest my head on my arm. "Goodbye, Gabriel," I whisper. More gulping sobs escape. I don't know if they'll ever stop. My heart is shattered beyond repair. It sucks to do the right thing.

I turn away from the view and lie down on the bench, curled up on my side, done with the real world. I need sleep, but my eyes are so gritty it hurts to close them. Dark bleakness seeps through me, draining my energy, and I finally calm into a cold numbness.

A few minutes later, a murmur of excitement ripples through the people nearby. They're gathering near my side of the ferry, and I sit up to see what the fuss is about. Maybe some dolphins are playing in the waves. What I wouldn't give for a distraction.

It's a yacht racing toward us, blaring its horn.

"It's the royal yacht!" someone exclaims.

I peer closer at the captain's perch. It's not Gabriel at the wheel. Geez, that yacht is driving so close it might ram into us.

"Anna Hebert!"

I look around wildly, my heart in my throat. I know that voice. He came for me. What does this mean? What did he do?

"Where are you?" I holler.

And then I hear a splash and an audible gasp from the ferry passengers. Oh my God. Gabriel just dove into the water!

He's swimming with sure strokes toward the ferry. He's crazy! What if the ferry propeller chops him up?

"Gabriel!" I scream at the top of my lungs. "Go back to

your boat!" He can't hear me and keeps going, quickly gaining on the ferry. He's shirtless, swimming in his boxer briefs. My God.

"Someone save the crown prince!" I holler, running to get a crew member. "Man overboard!"

A life preserver is thrown out to him, and then the crew member dives in to assist. Gabriel says something to him and takes the life preserver. The crew man signals up to another crew member to pull him in. Gabriel is directed to a ladder, and they both ascend.

My hands fly to my mouth at the sight of Gabriel, the crown prince of Villroy, striding purposefully toward me, soaking wet from head to toe *in his underwear*. In public. He might as well be naked, the blue boxer briefs outlining his bulge clearly. I swallow hard because even in his underwear he exudes power. He looks like a warrior, his golden skin glistening with drops of water, those magnificent strong shoulders, defined pecs and abs, narrow hips, long muscular thighs. The crowd fades back, giving us space, all eyes on him.

He stops in front of me, pulls my hands from my mouth, and growls, "I told you to stay put."

"What're you doing?" I grab him and hug him. His skin is chilled from the sea. "You're cold. You're crazy. What're you doing?"

He cups my face. "I'm getting my future bride. I choose you, Anna. If I can't marry you, I'll abdicate the throne."

The crowd gasps.

"Gabriel!" This is wrong. He can't do this.

He glances over at our audience, now holding up their phones, snapping pictures and probably video too. "Let's go somewhere more private." He grabs my hand and pulls me to the captain's command center at the top of the ferry. After a brief discussion, more like a barked series of orders from the crown prince, a lifeboat is lowered for us, and we're rowed back to the yacht.

Gabriel leads me to his private quarters, a bedroom suite, where he dries off and dresses. His eyes never leave mine the whole time he dresses, like he's afraid I'm going to bolt. I'm standing equidistant between the bed and him, where he put me. Of course I won't bolt. I have to convince him not to do this. Every part of me yearns for him, yet I know I can't let him abdicate.

He finishes dressing, grabs me by the shoulders, and looks into my eyes. "I love you." He says it almost like a challenge.

"I love you too, but—"

"No. That is enough."

"There's more at stake here and you know it. I left to make it easier for you to do the right thing."

"And you don't get to make that decision for me."

I pull away, wringing my hands together. "Be reasonable. Think about it."

"I have thought it through. I've talked to Phillip and he's willing to step into my place. He wants my happiness and has no hard feelings about the sudden change."

My stupid heart does a happy dance. I hadn't expected that. I thought whoever got roped into Gabriel's place wouldn't be happy about it. I'm sure it's not an easy job. But then Gabriel would lose out on his birthright, the role he's sacrificed a carefree childhood, his freedom, to prepare for. "Is that what you really want? Phillip as king?"

He's quiet for a moment, and I know deep down he doesn't want that at all.

"Gabriel," I choke out over the lump in my throat. My heart is breaking all over again because he is willing to sacrifice everything for me, and I simply can't allow it. I can't take that from him.

"I want you," he says quietly. "Because I do, my father has requested you go immediately to see him."

My hand goes to my throat. "I've been summoned by the king? Does he know the queen threw me in the dungeon?" My imagination goes wild with what the king might do, knowing I've corrupted his son with my lie and made him want to break with royal tradition. My mind flashes to a quick sham legal trial with a jury of the king's choosing leading directly to my execution. Old-school public-square style. Definitely death by guillotine.

He pulls me into his arms and lets out a sigh so big it parts my hair. "He's not going to harm you." My horrified expression must've given me away.

"Are you sure?" I ask his chest.

"Yes. He knows everything. He wants to hear it directly from you. I think he's trying to understand."

A nightlight-sized ray of hope glows in me. "So he wants to give me a chance?"

"I think so. My mother is not in favor, though. It's not a sure thing. They must be in agreement." He kisses me gently, leads me to the bed, and sits next to me. Then he tries to prepare me for his father's state of mind—the similarities between Gabriel falling for me and his uncle falling for an American. His father is still mad that he had the role of king forced on him, and doesn't want that for his own children. Gabriel is the chosen one, the only one his father has faith in.

"Oh, Gabriel, I feel like I've ruined everything."

"No, you saved me. You jolted me back to life from a dull zombie existence."

I give him a small watery smile. "A little like Frankenstein."

He widens his eyes and sticks his arms straight out. "Grr…"

I nearly laugh at this new playful side of Gabriel, but the weight of his future weighs too heavily on me to manage it. His arms go around me as he nuzzles into my neck. I can't find the strength to push him away. Instead I lean into him, warmed by the man I love with every cell in my being.

16

_____

Anna

We arrive at the port in Villroy to a crowd of locals with their phones up to record the event. News must've traveled fast from the ferry. Gabriel drops a protective arm around my shoulders, keeping me tight against him. Four security guards flank us, shielding us from the crowd, and hustle us into a Mercedes, whisking us back to the palace.

My hands are clammy, my nerves shot at the prospect of meeting the king. I've had very little sleep thanks to my night with Gabriel, my eyes are bloodshot from crying, my skin splotchy, and my hair is a wild frizzy mess from the sea breeze during my ferry ride. I can't believe Gabriel didn't mention how unpresentable I look. I got a scare when I finally checked my look in the mirror on the yacht ride back. I tried to fix myself up, but even I, a certified beautician, can't perform miracles. I'm a hot mess in a leopard dress—hey, that rhymes! I'm delirious. Perfect for meeting Gabriel's father—the freaking king of Villroy—for the first time ever.

"Are you going in with me to see the king?" I ask as

Gabriel escorts me inside the palace. There's a tremor in my voice. I wish I could pull off cool and in command the way Gabriel does.

His expression is completely neutral, shoulders back, walking with brisk confidence toward my doom. "Yes. Tell me more about your idea for the beauty product line based on Villroy's resources."

He's distracting me, and I'm grateful. I don't want to screw up with the king because of nerves. I babble on and on about potential local ingredients and their uses—seaweed, sea salt, algae, fish oil, sponges, even mud—and he listens attentively.

Long minutes later, I have no idea where we are in the palace, and I trail off. We must be in the most private royal quarters. I tense, my stomach doing a slow roll.

"Go on," he urges. "What inspired you to think of the cosmetics line?"

"I guess it was Villroy. I never thought of anything like that before."

He shifts to stand in front of me, gazing into my eyes as he lifts my hand and kisses my knuckles. My breath hitches at the intensity of his gaze.

He smiles. "I'm starting to see where Anna peeked at me through the Polly impersonation."

"Yes! That's what I was saying before. I was as much myself with you as I could be without putting Polly in jeopardy."

He gives my hand a squeeze. "You belong here. You belong with me."

Hot tears sting my eyes. "Gabriel, please, let's not jump to—"

"We're here." He steps forward and knocks on the

door. I hadn't realized we were standing right outside the king's private room. I would've kept my voice down.

A maid opens the door, does a quick curtsy, and steps aside.

I follow Gabriel in. His mother sits next to her husband's bed, her gaze on their joined hands. I see immediately the king's terrible condition. He has a large wide-shouldered build similar to Gabriel's, but he's too thin, shrunken and pale. Gabriel's ascension to the throne will happen very soon. The significance of Gabriel making the right choice is staring me right in the face.

I bow my head to the king and curtsy. "Your Majesty, thank you for seeing me."

I turn and do the same for the queen. "Thank you, Your Majesty."

I'm not sure which of them I was supposed to acknowledge first. It doesn't matter. They both look down their noses at me like I'm a cockroach trying to climb up the throne.

I ease back a step. Gabriel's large hand immediately pushes against my lower back in a show of support, or to keep me from bolting, I'm not sure.

A tense silence descends. I've been summoned, and I dare not speak further and blurt the wrong thing. The king must have something on his mind.

Finally, the king speaks. "Gabriel is the right leader for Villroy."

"I couldn't agree more," I say immediately.

"Good," the queen says. "Then we have an understanding."

Gabriel's voice growls from behind me, a rough authority to it that has me standing straighter. "Let me remind you that when this competition first began as your own version of a reality show, you said fresh blood with fresh ideas was needed to ensure a future for the kingdom. Anna has both. Her idea for helping Villroy may just save us. The fact that she's not royal matters nothing to me."

"What idea is that?" the king asks.

Gabriel squeezes my shoulder, silently urging me to speak.

I'm so nervous, the stakes are so high, I can barely get out the words. "It's a weeklong royal fantasy experience for women or maybe for a honeymooning couple."

Gabriel speaks in an animated voice. "It's more than that. There's room for expansion on the idea, a full spa could be built for day-trippers from the Continent, and a cosmetics line with native ingredients could be used at the spa and sold to guests. Think of the employment opportunities for construction, staff for a spa, small-scale manufacturing—"

"Even the fishermen could get involved." I can't help but interrupt because now I'm getting excited about the idea again. "They could gather seaweed, sponges, grow algae, or extract fish oil. There's a lot you can do with high-end cosmetics. And if the day spa is a success, along with the beauty product line, you could close the palace again and reserve the royal fantasy suite for special guests. Or maybe even use it as a fun bonus for the servants!"

They all stare at me. I clamp my mouth shut.

Gabriel shifts to meet my eyes. "Your ideas are brilliant. I can already see a way forward, working carefully in stages to the ultimate goal of a new sustainable industry for the fishermen."

My chest expands with pride. "Thank you."

The queen waves a hand dismissively. "Francesca's

idea was better. She understands the traditional history of Villroy."

"Francesca offers more of the same," Gabriel snaps. "And that's beside the point."

The king studies me for a long moment, his sharp aquamarine blue eyes assessing, and I try not to squirm. Finally, he asks, "Who are your people?"

"She's part French," Gabriel answers for me. "The islanders will like that."

I shake my head. I need them to know what they're getting with me. "I'm an orphan, Your Majesty. I've never asked anyone for anything. Everything I've gotten has been through my own hard work. Only recently I found out I had any people at all."

"Who are your people?" the king asks impatiently.

"Polly. She's my sixth cousin. We have a great-great-great-great-great-grandfather in common. My father's family was part of an emigration to Louisiana from Beaumont during a revolution there in the 1800s. She found me on the AncestryWise website, looking for an American family member for her undercover life."

Gabriel shifts me to face him. "Anna, why didn't you tell me this before? You have royal blood."

"Polly says it doesn't count. I'm too distant. It's like one drop."

"She's right," the queen says, sounding victorious. "Anna is still a commoner."

Gabriel wraps an arm around my shoulders, pulling me against his side so the two of us are facing the king together. "She is what Villroy needs." He gazes down at me with so much love in his eyes, I instantly choke up. "And what I need too."

I blink back tears. I can feel myself caving, but I need

to be strong for Gabriel. I force myself to turn to the king and queen and try one last time to save Gabriel's place. "I love him enough to let him go. It would break my heart, but I understand his value to the kingdom."

"Dammit, Anna," Gabriel starts, but the king cuts him off.

"Here is how it's going to be." His voice catches, and he has a violent coughing fit.

The queen grabs a glass of water nearby and offers it to him.

Tense seconds tick by while we wait for the king's coughing to abate. The queen looks pained and worried. I understand better the dark place she's coming from, watching him suffering like this.

I give Gabriel a small sideways squeeze. I know it's hard on him too. He's probably spent the most time with his father, more than any of his siblings, since Gabriel is the one who had to be taught what was expected of him as king.

Finally, his father is able to speak again. "Gabriel must remain heir to the throne. To avoid another replay of what happened with my brother's abdication of the throne, I grant permission for Gabriel to marry Anna."

The queen's jaw drops.

Gabriel grabs me in a crushing hug, wrapping me in his love. I'd shout my exultation, but I can barely draw breath. I'm beaming, though, warmth radiating through me, my heart drumming in my chest. He loosens his hold, and I let out a whoop that has my new in-laws staring at me, the queen in open disapproval. It occurs to me she hasn't spoken yet. Could she still call it off?

The king goes on in a formal tone, all business. "We will announce she's American, but her people are originally from French Beaumont, and she's a blood relative of the Beaumont princess. This will please the islanders." It's all technically true. He turns to his wife. "Do this for me, Alexandra."

Gabriel tenses beside me. I hold my breath.

She presses her lips together and nods once. I suck in air. *Yes!* The love between them is palpable, and I know it must be why they're allowing Gabriel to marry me. They understand love.

Gabriel hugs me again and then turns to his parents. "Thank you. You won't regret it. You've made the right choice."

"I don't need you to tell me that," his father says. "It's written all over your love-addled face."

The queen recovers herself and tells her husband, "She's completely unprepared for her role."

The king smiles with a wicked glint in his eye. "Then you must educate her."

The queen slowly turns to me with a look of horror. "Do you wish to be queen?"

"I wish to be Gabriel's wife."

"His wife will be queen."

"Then yes. But I have a lot to take care of back home first. I'm a beautician and a super. That's like a handy-woman. I can fix most anything."

Her eyes practically roll back in her head. "Oh, Lord."

I go over and hug my new mother-in-law, and then I hug my new father-in-law too. "I love your son. I love this place with all its history and traditions. It's the kind of permanent strong foundation I've always wanted. I will put all of my efforts into preserving it. Thank you for making me part of your family. I've wanted a family my whole life."

The queen closes her eyes for a moment and nods once, seeming touched by my sentiment. The king pats my hand, smiling warmly.

Gabriel does a deep formal bow to them both, which they acknowledge with a slight head incline, and then he grabs my hand and walks me toward the door.

"Bye, Your Royal Majesties," I call over my shoulder. "Can't wait to start queen lessons."

"Dear God," his mother says loud enough to carry.

The king just laughs. I think he likes me.

As soon as we get into the hallway, Gabriel grabs me in a hug, lifting me off the ground and spinning me around. "You were amazing. Completely pulled them to your side."

I beam at him. "I only told them the truth."

"Which was exactly what they needed to hear." He sets me back on my feet and kisses me, a swift hard kiss. "You really are a knight-ess in shining armor. You saved the prince."

"And I saved a princess too." I brandish an imaginary sword, and he laughs. I love to see him so happy. I am, too, giddy with it. My limbs are light, my heart so full I could float away from sheer joy.

"What's next for your knightly acts?" He winks. "I have some ideas."

I go up on tiptoe and kiss him. "I've got to get to work. Give me a tour of this place. I have to figure out where the royal fantasy suite should go."

"As you wish. We might have to test out a few places if it'll be used for a honeymoon suite too."

"Of course! We—ah!" He just tossed me over his shoulder!

His big hand clamps on my ass, and he's hustling me

down the hall. Next thing I know, we're in a bedroom. He kicks the door closed, sets me on my feet, and before I can check out the room for fantasy-suite potential, he's got me pinned against the wall.

He flashes a wolfish smile before he lifts me, his mouth devouring mine. I wrap my arms and legs around him and kiss him back passionately.

His hand slips up my dress, snagging on the string of my thong. "Honeymoon suite needs testing," he says against my lips before giving the thong a sharp tug, ripping it. His fingers slide inside me, pumping into me as his thumb strums an orgasmic tune. "Test, test, test."

My head arches back as pleasure floods my body. "Yes!" And then there are no words. I'm panting, hurtling toward release, mindlessly writhing against his hand. Everything in me coils tight. His mouth covers mine just as I peak, swallowing my harsh cry, easing me back to earth. Once I stop moaning, he sets me back on my feet.

I'm floating in a pleasant haze, eyes closed, leaning lazily back against the wall while Gabriel does whatever. I assume he's stripping. I slowly become aware long minutes have passed, and open my eyes. He strides toward me, gloriously naked, condom on.

"Wow." I'm about to make a joke about the abundance of condoms in the royal guest rooms, but that's as far as I get because he's on me. He lifts me up and takes me in one swift thrust. I gasp at the sudden invasion, a shockwave of pleasure rippling through me. He's hot and thick, an exquisite ache.

He stills, deep inside me, his hand coming up to hold my head, his eyes burning into mine. "Anna."

I love hearing my real name. I love the passion, love

the intensity, just plain love our love. "I love you, Gabriel."

He kisses me tenderly. "I love you, my queen."

"You're the most amazing man I've ever met."

His thumb strokes my cheek, his voice rough. "And you are my heart."

I blink back tears that quickly vanish as Gabriel's mouth covers mine, his hips pumping slow and deep into me. Within minutes, the slow tenderness morphs into heart-pounding primal fucking, the wall at my back, Gabriel's hard body against my front. My world narrows down to the heat in Gabriel's eyes, his hands gripping my hips, his deep powerful thrusts carrying me higher and higher. A throaty cry rips from my throat, my body clamping down on him as I climax, and then he goes over with a harsh guttural groan.

I go limp, sated and relaxed. He shifts his hold on me, banding an arm around my lower back, keeping me in place between him and the wall.

I smile what I'm sure is a huge goofy grin. "This room totally works for a honeymoon suite."

He cradles my jaw and kisses me, gentler now, but thorough, like he can't stop kissing me. I'm drunk on it, drunk on him.

Long moments later, he lifts his head. "There might be a better choice. We'll have to continue our search for the perfect spot. It could take a while. This is a big palace."

I rock against him. "I'll say."

He smiles against my mouth, kisses me again deeply, and I'm home for good.

EPILOGUE

Anna

"You're free!" I grab Polly in the backseat of the rented Hummer with tinted windows and hug her fiercely. We've just come from her trial. No jail time, woo-hoo!

She pulls back and smiles at me warmly. "All thanks to you, cousin." She turns to Gabriel. "And you too. Thank you so much for your help. And your discretion."

My cousin is the height of royal manners. I see it now in the way she holds herself, the way she speaks more formally to Gabriel, one royal to another. And my wonderful princely fiancé pulled every string he had to get Polly a fantastic lawyer and to keep it all quiet.

Gabriel smiles. "I was happy to help, though I'm afraid you still have the probation tying you here."

"I don't mind," Polly says. "I need some time away from home. Now I have twelve months of mandatory time away. I've told my parents I'm getting my MBA. They're all for education." She turns to me. "Sorry we lost the apartment building."

I wave that away. "Don't even worry about it! It was

the thought that counted. You wanted to give me a generous gift, and that means so much. I'm just sorry you lost the money you paid for it." The judge ruled that the deed to the building return to its original owner, and then Polly's payment was forfeited to the government.

"I'm fine," she says. "Now that I'm in touch with my family again, all is well. Okay, maybe I told a tiny white lie about getting my MBA, which, come to think of it, I should've went with in the first place instead of this elaborate undercover story."

"Your story was much more interesting," I assure her. "Exciting, right?"

She laughs. "It was! I had great fun right up until the arrest."

We both laugh. Gabriel smiles and shakes his head.

"You should get an MBA," I tell her. "You're here anyway. I think you can get one online even."

"Maybe I will," she says brightly. "It can only help with the tourism industry back home."

I give her a fist bump.

"I'll miss you, Anna," she says. "I'm coming to visit you in Villroy just as soon as my probation is up."

"Absolutely! And you have Mike here to visit with." She's visited my foster dad regularly, checking in on him. She said he was a great comfort to her during the stressful time while I was gone.

"Actually, Mike offered to let me stay with him if I was granted probation," she says. "I'm not sure if I should take him up on the offer. I mean, I want to, he's been so kind, but I know he's not feeling well, and I don't want to impose."

I breathe a sigh of relief. "That's wonderful. You should definitely take him up on that offer. He's used to having a houseful of people. He fostered a lot of kids for so many years. And I would feel so much better knowing he has you for company now that I'm moving to Villroy."

Gabriel and I spent the past two weeks here in Tampa, wrapping up loose ends at work and at my apartment, but mostly visiting Mike. He's in stable condition and is really happy about my engagement. He approves of Gabriel, which means the world to me because I know Mike always has my best interests at heart. Gabriel offered to let him live at the palace with us, but he prefers to stay in his familiar home. So Gabriel did the next best thing and made arrangements for Mike's nurse to move in for full-time care. Between that and Polly living with him, I can rest easy. I'll still visit, of course, and call and text and email. He's my dad.

"Okay, then it's settled." Polly elbows me. "Mike says I remind him of an overly polite version of you."

"Ha! You've got a ways to go to get to my level of…" I turn to Gabriel. "What is it you call me?"

"Brash."

"Yes, brash. That's his overly polite way of saying rude."

Gabriel gives my hand a squeeze. "Not rude. Bold and impertinent, but never rude. You treat people with respect."

"She does," Polly says. "I'm so glad we found each other, even if for just a few months. And I'm so glad you two found each other! Anna, can you imagine if I were the one who went to Villroy to compete for Gabriel's hand?"

"Thank God you weren't allowed to leave the state!" I exclaim. "You might've stolen my future husband!"

Gabriel shakes his head. "You're not that similar. There's just a family resemblance."

Polly takes out her hair clip and shakes out her curly hair. We go cheek to cheek, smiling at Gabriel. "See?" she says.

"Twins," I say.

"I'm seeing double," he says, leaning in toward Polly. "Give me a kiss, darling, so I know it's you."

"Gabriel!"

He grins and swerves at the last moment to kiss the right woman. Me.

~

Two weeks later at the royal ball...

Gabriel

Some people say I rushed into things with Anna. Those people are wrong. I've been waiting my whole life for her, and now that she's here, I can't wait to start our life together. I'm the first to admit she's a unique addition to the family, outspoken and not always aware of the proper protocol. Still, you can't help but love her; even the queen has warmed up to her most eager student. After wrapping things up at home, Anna spent the last two weeks working very closely with my mother, learning our traditions and royal expectations. They planned this ball together to celebrate our engagement.

Anna's floor-length gown is emerald green. A halter top goes up to her neck, revealing no cleavage but fitting perfectly to her curves. Her wild dark curls are pulled away from her face by a glittering diamond headband, the length of her hair cascading down her back. The princesses from the barbaric competition were invited—

Anna's idea. They all declined, as I predicted. They don't want their noses rubbed in their loss. All of my family is here and many of the nobility, who've long been friendly with Villroy.

I watch Anna follow my mother around, greeting guests. She's irresistibly charming in her bubbly vivacious way. In more good news, my father seems reinvigorated by our upcoming wedding. He wants to be there to see it. Anna visits him daily, entertaining him with stories of her clients back home and all of their quirks. He finds her "refreshing." She even gave him a haircut. Only Anna would've dared ask.

I cross the room to reclaim her, having waited long enough for her queen-in-training routine with my mother. "May I have this dance?"

She beams at me and does a graceful curtsy. "I'd love that!" She can't contain her natural enthusiasm, and I never want her to. I love that about her.

I crook my arm and guide her to the dance floor. The orchestra smoothly transitions to a slow song. I wrap an arm around her waist, take her hand, and lead her in a slow box step. More couples join us.

She feels up my shoulder. "Have I mentioned how handsome you look in a tux?"

"You have, but feel free to mention it again."

She squeezes my bicep. "Outrageously handsome. Are you having a good time? I haven't seen you crack a smile. You probably didn't notice, but I've been secretly spying on you from across the room."

"I'm having a good time now."

She hugs me in her spontaneous way before returning to our dance position. I can't remember ever feeling so loved. Her brown eyes sparkle at me the way they do when she has an idea.

"What?"

She flashes a smile. "I was thinking since it takes two more *long* months to plan a proper royal wedding—"

"Which is as short a time as I could make it."

"Yes, I know you can't wait to tie me down. Ha! Remember—"

"Shh, darling." I pull her close and whisper in her ear, "Of course I remember tying you down, but if you start talking about that here, you're going to get me in an *unseemly* state just thinking about it."

"Unseemly." She fights back a laugh and loses. She looks up at me, flushed pink and smiling. "Oh, Gabriel, sometimes you just come out with the funniest things." She kisses my cheek and resumes our dance. "Anyway, the renovation on our royal fantasy guest suite should be done by the time our wedding finally rolls around, knock on wood—" she knocks on her head "—and I think we should spend our wedding night there to try it out."

"Done."

"You're so easygoing!"

I'm not. I never have been, but I'll do anything for her. She's given up her home, her career, her dream to own her own salon, and her privacy. I will do anything and everything in my power to bring her happiness in the new life she's chosen with me.

I cradle her face with one hand and kiss her. She throws her arms around my neck and returns the kiss enthusiastically. When she finally lets me up for air, she glances around, noticing all eyes are on us. She quickly wipes the edges of my lips, probably rubbing off her red lipstick.

"I forgot," she whispers, "public displays of affection are frowned upon."

"It's our engagement party. What better time to celebrate our love?"

She beams at me. "I love you, Gabriel Rourke."

"And I love you, Anna Hebert soon-to-be Rourke."

She sighs happily. "Did I tell you I've already booked a ladies' week in the new royal guest suite?"

"No. What if it's not ready?"

"I'll jump in with my own tool belt if I have to. But I'm not worried. I'll be supervising all the contractors personally."

"Okay, and who are the lucky guests?"

"My best wealthiest clients back home. They're coming for a week for beauty treatments by me—hair, nails, facials." She lowers her voice conspiratorially. "They're very attached to me. The relationship with your hairdresser is sacred."

"I was not aware of that."

"Oh, yeah, for sure." She nods vigorously. "Though, to be perfectly honest, the bigger draw for the ladies is a royal bachelor auction. They can win a date with a prince!"

I suppress my horror. It sounds worse than the barbaric bridal games my mother concocted. And the princes must be my brothers. Who else would agree to it? Anna has won them all over.

"Ta-dah!" she exclaims. "That's my next fundraising idea. You know we need to keep the ball rolling. We want to move forward with my day spa idea and natural cosmetics line."

When she says we, she means the two of us. "We do.

So…do my brothers know they're going to be auctioned off?"

She scans the room for them, wiggling her fingers when she spots them gathered near the bar. She blows them a kiss before turning back to me. "Nope. They have no clue. I'm sure they'll do it for me."

"They will. They love you just like everyone in my family."

She gives me a sweet smile and squeezes my arm. "The truth is, I think it's the royal hottie who'll draw the most bids. He's got quite the internet following. It's perfect!"

I glance over at poor unsuspecting Phillip, smiling and laughing without a care in the world as usual. Then I remember how he knew all about the bridal competition before it happened and didn't say a word about it to warn me. In fact, when he finally showed his face, he seemed amused by the whole undignified ordeal thrust upon me.

I turn back to Anna. "You're brilliant. Make sure I'm there when you tell him."

Her brows furrow together. "Why? Do you think he'll be upset?"

"He'll be something."

She slowly nods, like *message received*. "I'll wait until the last possible minute."

I can't help my smile. "That sounds perfect." Now that Anna's here, things will never be stuffy and boring at the palace again.

Don't miss the next book in the series *Royal Hottie*, where Phillip unexpectedly finds himself the prime draw in a bachelor auction!

Royal Hottie

Phillip

I never expected to be the prime target of a bachelor auction, compliments of my outrageous sister-in-law, the new queen. I don't care if the internet has turned me into a royal hottie meme, I am not a piece of meat. So when the first eager single woman arrives at the palace, I send her packing. Only the damn woman refuses to leave.

Ruby

Why would I want to buy a date with an arrogant rude prince? I'm here to do a job, which I desperately need, and no delusional prince is going to stand in my way. Obviously, the "royal hottie" believes the hype.

So how did I end up winning the top prize in a royal bachelor auction, and what will I do with him?

I can't let myself fall for a playboy. Besides, we're heading in opposite directions. He's going on an international tour for a year or more, and I absolutely have to get back to the US. Only this prince is used to getting what he wants, and now he wants me.

Sign up for my newsletter to be emailed when *Royal Hottie* releases at kyliegilmore.com/newsletter

ALSO BY KYLIE GILMORE

Happy Endings Book Club Series

Hidden Hollywood (Book 1)

Inviting Trouble (Book 2)

So Revealing (Book 3)

Formal Arrangement (Book 4)

Bad Boy Done Wrong (Book 5)

Mess With Me (Book 6)

Resisting Fate (Book 7)

Chance of Romance (Book 8)

Wicked Flirt (Book 9)

An Inconvenient Plan (Book 10)

A Happy Endings Wedding (Book 11)

The Clover Park Series

The Opposite of Wild (Book 1)

Daisy Does It All (Book 2)

Bad Taste in Men (Book 3)

Kissing Santa (Book 4)

Restless Harmony (Book 5)

Not My Romeo (Book 6)

Rev Me Up (Book 7)

An Ambitious Engagement (Book 8)

Clutch Player (Book 9)

A Tempting Friendship (Book 10)

Clover Park Bride: A Clover Park Short

A Valentine's Day Gift (Book 11)

Maggie Meets Her Match (Book 12)

The Clover Park STUDS Series

Almost Over It (Book 1)

Almost Married (Book 2)

Almost Fate (Book 3)

Almost in Love (Book 4)

Almost Romance (Book 5)

Almost Hitched (Book 6)

The Rourkes Series

Royal Catch (Book 1)

Royal Hottie (Book 2)

Royal Darling (Book 3)

Royal Charmer (Book 4)

Royal Player (Book 5)

Royal Shark (Book 6)

ABOUT THE AUTHOR

Kylie Gilmore is the *USA Today* bestselling author of the Rourkes series, the Happy Endings Book Club series, the Clover Park series, and the Clover Park STUDS series. She writes humorous romance that makes you laugh, cry, and reach for a cold glass of water.

Kylie lives in New York with her family, two cats, and a nutso dog. When she's not writing, wrangling kids, or dutifully taking notes at writing conferences, you can find her flexing her muscles all the way to the high cabinet for her secret chocolate stash.

Thanks for reading *Royal Catch*. I hope you enjoyed it. Would you like to know about new releases? You can sign up for my new release email list at kyliegilmore.com/newsletter. I promise not to clog your inbox! Only new release info, sales, and some fun giveaways.

I love to hear from readers! You can find me at:
kyliegilmore.com
Instagram.com/kyliegilmore
Facebook.com/KylieGilmoreToo
Twitter @KylieGilmoreToo

If you liked Gabriel and Anna's story, please leave a review on your favorite retailer's website or Goodreads. Thank you.

9 781942 238843